Ride a
COCK HORSE

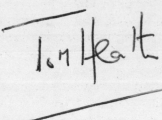

Gillian Mears was born in 1964 and grew up with her three sisters in North Coast towns of NSW. In Sydney she abandoned an Arts/Archaeology degree to work as a lab assistant and waitress. In 1985 she completed a Communications degree at the NSW Institute of Technology. She is now living in Grafton in an old shingle house with an overgrown garden. *Ride a Cock Horse* is her first book.

Ride a
COCK HORSE

Gillian
MEARS

First published 1988
by Pascoe Publishing Pty Ltd
P.O. Box 51, Fairfield 3078
Australia

Ride a Cock Horse
ISBN 0–947 087 12 5

Printed in Australia by
The Book Printer
Maryborough
Typeset in Palatino by Bookset

Cover art and book design by Stephen Pascoe

Contents

Acknowledgements

The following stories were previously published. 'The Midnight Shift' in *Australian Short Stories* no 13, 1986 and *Hecate* vol XI no 2 1985. 'Dwarfed' in *Fling* vol 5 no 1 1985. 'Nappy Change' in *Thirteen New Beginnings: an anthology* Local Consumption Publishers 1987. 'Looping the Loop' in *Hecate* vol XII no's 1/2 1986.

The quotation in Old Age Fairies is from *The Hoofs of the Horses* by Will H Ogilvie printed in *The Collected Sporting Verse of Will H Ogilvie* published in London by Constable & Co, 1932.

A Prophet's Thumb

Sss, sss, sss, the men sounded deadly and wielded imaginary whips. Beetle lifted his leg at the bottom of one pair of trousers but nobody yelled or noticed. Albert laughed secretly and pressed on to be within sight of the finishing post.

Doom, doom, went the hoofbeats and Albert could feel the ground shake. He scooted through a forest of tall legs. Far above, hissing men in hats and the yellow summer sky. *Doom, doom.* The hoofbeats trembled closer and filled him up. Albert could feel them thudding straight into his heart.

'They're coming!' Albert shrieked. 'Come on Beetle.'

Clear of the crowd, light bounced. Albert blinked to see the horses heaving before the straight. The track was luminous, was alive with the ripple of racing silks. Dust flew. The horses came like thunder. There was a storminess; in the cries of the crowd; in the yellow clouds. To catch sight of his favourite, Albert leapt up and down.

'Go it girl,' he hugged himself tightly as he recognized the big bay mare he'd bet Jinnie would lead all the way. From where he stood, she looked a certainty. Then suddenly it came to Albert that she was yawing into the straight all wrong. Clear of the inside-rail-jostling, she was way too wide.

'No,' whispered Albert. He'd picked her out in the saddling enclosure as the winner. Her long, pretty ears had made him smile and the way she tried to nip the jockey.

'Go it girl . . .' Albert clutched Beetle so hard, the puppy whimpered. Before the race, his favourite had flicked her ears back and forth like she knew what the trainer was telling the jockey. 'Oh please turn.' Beetle wriggled free and was lost in the maze of legs. On tip toes, Albert watched the railings of light wood splinter and split into the bay mare. At the last minute, she tried to leap. The jockey spiralled into the air. The mare's back legs tangled in a mess of timber and she hit the ground heavily. *Ssss, ssss.* The urging noises of the men lost momentum. The rest of the field galloped past the post but Albert was sure he felt her fall: the muffled thump: the snap-snap of her legs through wood. Somewhere, out of sight, Beetle was yapping and yapping.

Albert ran to where people were milling round the jockey. Clouds covered the sun. The purple and gold patchwork of the jockey silks didn't gleam anymore. When Albert glanced over to the horse he felt his fright shrivelling and contracting. It shrank and shrank into a cold knot of panic. The jockey's cap lay upside down in a mess of busted up palings. Soon Old Fatgut McPhee, the vet, would arrive at the accident. Under the ricketty grandstand, Albert thought he could see Old Fatgut exchanging money with someone before starting to waddle across.

There was blood. When Albert turned back to the fallen mare, Beetle was there. He was snuffling in the dust for the wild red smell. The blood was seeping in a criss cross of little cuts. 'Beetle,' Albert called. Beetle wagged his tail. 'Beetle!' The puppy wriggled nervously, sniffing and yelping. Albert made a grab but Beetle shot round to the far side of the horse, making her eyes roll and quiver. Albert approached slowly. He turned his eyes into chinaman slits to make the crowd of people near the jockey grow smaller and smaller. If Albert concentrated, he could make anything he liked vanish. Even Beetle disappeared. He let the fallen mare fill his vision.

'You'll be alright,' Albert crouched down to be near. 'Only a few cuts. Old Fatgut'll fix you up. He'll be along,' Albert tried to talk over the snuffling noises of

8

blood in her nostrils. 'Old Fatgut. He's pretty good. You know that.' The bridle was torn down over her face, flattening one ear. Albert wanted to fix it up. The other untrapped ear was like a long fine shell. 'Hush-a-bye, hush-a-bye,' Albert said, like he'd heard his mother doing over the new baby. 'You'll be alright. In no time,' his fingers inched towards her face. She snorted. The blood sprayed a fine pattern onto Albert's face. He licked his lip to taste the delicate fright of pink. 'Don't do that,' Albert swallowed but the sensation of thin blood stuck in his throat and wouldn't go down. 'I was only trying to fix the bridle, get your ear out. That's why I bet Jinnie you'd win. Cause of your ears. You were the prettiest. You never had to go through the railings.' Albert checked her legs. They were fine and folded up — shiny with sweat or blood. He thrilled to be so close. The horses at home never stayed lying down. In the early mornings or on a really hot day, he'd try to sneak up on his father's two stockhorse geldings but as soon as he was within a few feet of them, they'd always groan and stand up. It was a different feeling to be at the same level. For the first time Albert could look right into a horse's eyes. He'd never realized they were so blue and sad looking in the middle. Was it because she was hurting so much? If he wobbled back on his heels, she grew frightened all over again and rolled her eyes. Then he noticed the messy, brown pigment, spreading into the scared white. 'Old Fatgut,' Albert murmured, because he'd run out of words. 'Old Fatgut will come.' She grunted and let her neck loll to the ground. The more Albert looked into her left eye, the worse he felt. Was it going milky? If only Old Fatgut would hurry.

The blood was trickling. Albert shut his eyes and thought he could hear it leaking from her. The dust was soaking it up. Listening to the blood made him more scared. Such a lonely sound he had to open his eyes. In the saddling enclosure, the mare had four white socks. Now the front one closest to Albert was stained and wet. The brilliant red colour held his gaze. Caught in the tuft of hair on her fetlock, the blood was thick, brighter than paint, frightening. Between her front legs, the dirt grew wet and smelt strong and strange. Albert tried to look somewhere else. He fingered his busted up thumbnail and said 'there, there; there there,' as if she just had a bit of colic like the new baby.

There were other people nearby. Albert tried to make them disappear but they were crowding too close. He couldn't keep them out.

'Get that little fella out of the way,' someone said. Albert felt a hand pulling him back. Beetle spun into sight, sniffing at all the strange ankles. To get anywhere close again, Albert edged round to the other side. He grabbed Beetle who only snuffled and wriggled all the more.

The staring people made the mare shudder. She tried to get up. She strained but her front legs seemed too spindly to support her. Albert stared in at the soft place under her legs that he hadn't been able to see before. A thick bit of timber was poking out. There was darker blood and it started spurting.

'She's done for by the looks of it,' pronounced Old Fatgut McPhee. Albert hadn't noticed his arrival. The vet bent down: so close Albert was able to spot the broken, purple veins in his face, fluttering like mauve January moths.

Old Fatgut shook his head. 'Won't be long, I shouldn't think,' he said as the mare trembled and again tried to stand. She sank back, the piece of railing pushed deeper in. Albert wished he hadn't watched. He didn't want to see her dying. He imagined the wood creaking deeper into her and blinked back some tears.

'Must've hit a lung,' said Fatgut. 'All that blood.' Albert turned his face up to the pale, pasty chin. From below the vet looked fatter than ever.

'Bloody ratbag anyway,' said a man in the crowd.

'Hold on girl,' Albert wanted to block his ears to the flying judgements.

'Shouldn't never of allowed her the run.'

'Almost did the same bloody thing a fortnight ago.'

'Mongrel of a mare. Could've killed the jock!'

Overhead, the explanations wheeled like the clouds.

'They don't know,' Albert told Beetle. 'They just wouldn't know.' He looked across to the grandstand and then beyond to the clearing under the gumtrees. Jinnie was there with Adelaine, walking round and round the main attraction of this race meeting. Not the saddling enclosure, not the horses or the tiny jockeys almost ready for the last race, but the flying machine that landed in the racecourse two days ago. The man in the stripey jacket, who flew the aeroplane, was taking every opportunity to charge people three shillings for a sit inside. Under the storm clouds, the metal of the machine was green and scarey. Albert hated it and his sisters for not even caring about the horse. With the appearance of the flying man in the blue and white coat people began to hurry across to hear him talk. The jockey was carried away on a stretcher and soon it was only Albert, Beetle and Old Fatgut the vet standing by the mare. Albert talked into her shy eyes, offering gentle encouragement, 'atta girl, atta girl. It's better now, without everyone. They've all gone off to see that stupid aeroplane again.' He wished he could run his fingers into the bony hollows above her eyes.

'A marvellous invention my boy.'

'Yes Mr McPhee,' Albert hoped Old Fatgut would leave too. It wasn't as if he was doing anything to help.

'Bit of bad luck,' said Old Fatgut to a thin man who'd walked up behind.

'She was looking for it,' the man said. He spat and began to strip off the bridle. Her ear came free and she flicked it weakly. The man dragged the bit over the mare's teeth. Not easing it out gently the way Albert's Dad did, with care and always telling the horses stories. 'Always talk to a horse,' Albert's Dad would say, 'they'll know what you mean,' and sometimes would

11

swing Albert up in front of him, saying, 'Now Topsy, it's only little Albert we're taking for a ride.'

The skinny man had to heave to get the saddle off and began swearing when the girth wouldn't come free.

'Just leave it Jack,' said Old Fatgut. 'You can get the bloody girth after. Jesus, you been drinking or something? Just leave it. Go on.'

The man made a noise like something being belted and went off with the racing pad flung over one shoulder.

'Bloody hayseed trainer that one,' said Old Fatgut. 'Used to call himself a jockey but never did any good. Too mean by half,' Old Fatgut touched Albert on the shoulder. 'You should go too y'know,' he said. 'Won't be a pretty sight. How about you have a look at that plane. Storm looks like it's giving us a miss. Only three shillings for a sit in the cabin. Heh? A Sopwith Biplane. You won't see one of those on the racecourse every day. See horses anytime. You might like to put something on the last race for me. Just have to see the bloke under the stand over there.'

Albert looked at the way the vet's trousers wrinkled at each knee. There was a thud when the mare's head hit the dirt. Her mane was thin, glossy, black, with dust caught in the ends of it. Albert perched on his heels to touch. His small fingers curled in the hair. If only he had a penknife he could have taken some. When he swept her mane right back he saw how much darker and shorter her coat was there. Where the sweat had dried was a salty, white crust. More sweat had gathered in a shallow indentation on her neck. Old Fatgut groaned downwards to be at Albert's level. He pushed his fat thumb against the small hollow. 'Meant to be lucky,' said Fatgut. 'Same as a horse that goes right over when it's rolling. But you'll find most of them are normally bigger than this one,' he took away his thumb and Albert saw how quite a bit of sweat had gathered inside.

'What is it?' Albert asked.

'They're called a Prophet's Thumb. It's some sort of abnormality before the horse is even born. Quite common, mostly in thoroughbreds.' Fatgut wobbled on his heels and had to steady himself on the side of the dead mare for balance. 'Meant to be lucky though.'

'Didn't bring her any luck,' Albert accused and wiped his face with the sleeve of his best shirt.

'No, I don't suppose it did,' said the vet. He was turning to go. 'And if I'm going to get lucky I'd better get something on this last race.'

Albert only stayed a moment longer. Long enough to pull back her mane again in order to see the sweaty dint, long enough to slide his thumb over her dead coat and see his thumb was the perfect fit. It formed an exact lid to the Prophet's Thumb that had brought her no luck at all. His thumb was a sort of cover. He kept it in place as though to do so would seal in the sadness creeping out to him. She still smelt alive. Not fair. Using his thumbnail he scraped away the dried sweat until her Prophet's Thumb looked glossy and bright and full of good fortune. It was the only way he could think of saying goodbye.

Beetle had curled himself into a ball, fast asleep in the erratic sunshine. Albert picked him up to breathe in his milky, sleepy smell. Jinnie and Adelaine were easy to find, listening to the man with the plane. He was reading from a small book.

'Flying caps and goggles,' declared the man, 'are unnecessary with the Sopwith Biplane. Sit at ease in the machine, your movements cannot possibly affect its balance . . .'

The light was falling in dislocated ribbons around the dead bay mare. Looking back, Albert half expected her to stand up, shaking and twitching to get rid of the dust, before settling down to have a pick of grass.

'Albert don't go doing that!' Adelaine pulled his thumb out of his mouth. 'And where do you think you've been.' She was snappy.

'You'll get rabbit teeth if you suck your thumb,' said Jinnie. 'We've already had a sit inside for half price.'

The last field of the day galloped past the busted up corner railings, into the straight. The mare was a bright bay shape that couldn't snort or prance to see the other horses passing. Albert put his thumb back to taste the stronger, saltier sweat. He remembered blood and blue eyes.

'Cry Baby,' screamed Jinnie, so everyone looked away from the plane at him. 'Thumbsucker,' she poked her tongue out. 'There's going to be joyrides. Tomorrow. But not for crybabies.'

There was a glassiness in the sky that hadn't stormed, in the gleaming jockeys riding circular west into the sun as they pulled their horses up. Albert kept sucking his thumb. Oddly enough, despite the unsweet flavour of horse sweat, it felt lucky to do so. Hadn't his thumb been the exact fit?

'Don't forget you owe me,' crowed Jinnie. 'Proper bet. I get your apple pie.'

Albert sucked hard, thinking his secret over and over, thinking lucky futures, as he pinched Jinnie as hard as he could and waited for Adelaine's smacks to start falling.

Nappy Change

After seeing for the first time his mother change a nappy, Albert knew he couldn't eat his favourite banana custard anymore. Not ever again. The stuff lying in the folds of a steaming napkin looked exactly the same only custard was served in the thick, white pudding plates from the cupboard. They shared the same lumps. The older the baby got the worse it smelt but all the same, something of a spectacle to watch a nappy being changed. You never could tell what would happen.

Albert watched his mother's hands unlatching the pins and the baby's napkin unfurling all on its own. He knelt on a chair for an elevated view. It was a mystery why the kitchen table must be used for such a job.

The mess nestled inside the nappy like the curds and whey toothless Mrs Wadge had to eat three times a day. Puddled. Not floating but almost.

His mother's fingers whisked in and out with the rag and ointment to stop the baby getting the chafes. She lifted the white and blue legs to clean it all up and Albert could see the baby's bottom. It wasn't fat in the least but pointed and cold looking.

Into the pail flew the dirty nappy. Much to Albert's disgust it was nearly a full bucket load. His newly assigned chore was to hose out the worst of the mess. He began to climb off the chair, clanking the nappy pail with his feet so it almost fell over. There was no warning for what was to come. Maybe he'd missed the straining and red faced signals. It exploded out with air and bits of yellow stuff flying all over the place. Not even his mother was prepared. Some just about hit the wall. The noise was louder than a grownup could do;

louder than Mr Clapperton with piles who was always popping air. Christopher Wetherstone Clark had a good word for windiness. Bombies. It was a word that made you laugh.

'Did I do projectile poos too Mum?' Albert craned to see his baby brother Sidney.

No reply. Safety pin between her teeth, she was repeating the cleaning up process. And when Sidney's little donger sprang into the air and began spouting, she moved quickly to complete the final fold and be finished. Despite the pee she didn't reach for a clean napkin. A wonder something didn't get pricked the way she jabbed the pin through the thick cloth. Albert couldn't get over that little donger. Practically the size of one of his own toes. So small and something not quite right with a thin purple line across the top.

Albert's chore couldn't be put off any longer. He grabbed the nappy pail without enthusiasm.

'Put your shoes on,' his mother sighed.

Outside the grass was spiky on his feet, the metal bucket cold where it banged against his leg. The nappies right at the bottom made him almost sick. The one at the top was very warm and wet. A calf with the white scours was cleaner by far. Maybe all that Sidney needed was a good dose of the calves' castor oil.

When all were done he dumped them into the cement laundry tub and scrubbed his hands with a block of lime. There had been thirteen. One up from Sunday and increasing all the time. Soon that part of the garden would outstink the chookhouse. The thought filled Albert with gloom and he ignored Bluey rolling over and over in front of him, hoping for a belly tickle.

The stage had been reached where Albert could smell the baby's poop all the time and Sidney was only seven and a half weeks old. It lingered on his hands, though he was extra careful to hold the nappies up by the end of a stick when hosing. In bed at night the smell seemed to rise around him from the sheets. Honey sandwiches

16

tasted strange which was a real problem because Miss Aimsley checked that everyone finished their lunch. There was only one solution: to stuff the sandwiches, dribbling and with butter turning sour, into your shirt until it was safe to throw them away. Down the dunny along with Tommy Amos' burnt chocolate slice and Christopher Wetherstone Clark's apples.

Perhaps a bit of one of little Sid's projectile efforts had flung itself into his nose and got stuck. Lodged itself forever amongst the bogeymen. A good reason to stop picking your nose and eating it. Better than one hundred slaps from mother or big sisters or Miss Aimsley.

One Thursday Evening

The calf had its legs so tangled in the rope that its head brushed the ground. Albert ran over to un-tether it and take it for a feed. Matilda and his mother were unpegging sheets from the line. As they swiftly folded, shadows swooped into corners. The air turned mauve and dull and smelt of coloured Christmas beetles in gum trees. Albert turned a few loose legged cart-wheels to reach the calf; in slow motion, trying to stay upside down for as long as possible. From over at the milking sheds floated sounds of the cows clattering into position on the cement cobbles. Albert tipped over one more time on his hands, keeping his eyes open to see if the grey verandah railings around the house looked any different. They didn't. It was dizzying to stop and stand upright, arms still in a tilt to catch the warm afternoon wind.

'Take the calf to be fed Albert,' Matilda perched the washing basket on her hip and turned to go.

'Yes Rattie Mattie,' shrieked Albert.

'Don't be rude to your sister,' his mother said and pounced on the baby crawling after the dog's tail. Little Sidney laughed fatly.

The calf was hungry, butting Albert all the way to the small paddock behind the dairy and pulling the thick halter rope through his fingers. Monty was in the sepa-rating room, pouring pails of milk into the new centrifu-gal separator. No-one except old Stanley Whiffler used the old system of allowing cream to rise in the big pans. It was slow and wasteful and besides that, the separa-tors weren't expensive.

'Hello Monty,' Albert tapped the separator. 'Going alright is it?'

'Not too bad. Not too bad.' Monty's lips were circled with white milk froth. He handed across a pail of separated milk for the calf. Albert crouched and crumbled in a softened linseed oil cake.

'Albert, you know what your Dad says about mixing calf food in here. You'll taint the cream and then you'll be in strife.' Monty was from England. Albert liked the soft notes in his voice. Picking up the full-to-the-brim bucket of milk, Albert shrugged and went outside.

The oil cake breaking through his fingers smelt strong and left his hands feeling butter smooth. That was what the oil was for — a supplement to replace the butter fat removed in the separator. It wasn't as tasty for the calves as whole milk but they soon got used to it. And easy teaching them to drink. For the first two weeks it was best to use milk warm and fresh from the mother. It took all five of Albert's fingers to get a calf sucking milk from a bucket. Monty's hands were so thick he only had to use his middle two. With small calves you dipped a hand into the milk and put it into the calf's mouth. Then, as the calf tasted the milk and began to suck, you slowly drew your hand down until the calf was gulping the milk on its own.

This calf was almost two months old and didn't need showing the way down to the milky bucket. All the same Albert stuck his fingers in to feel the greedy rhythm; the rough tongue; the ridges along the roof of the mouth.

This was nothing like the way Sidney lay buried in his mother's breast, which only the other day Albert noticed was ploughed up with purple welts and throbbing blue veins. Sometimes though, Sidney was nowhere near quick enough for the milk which squirted all by itself onto his mother's shirt. Albert had tried, when his mother was cooking, to stick his little finger into Sidney's mouth. But babies weren't smart like calves and Sidney had started to howl — in sharp bursts of sound the way he did after a bath. His mother had come

19

and changed another nappy and told Albert to stop forever pestering his new little brother.

The calf finished and tipped the bucket. Albert ran his fingers through thick whorls of underneck hair and yanked at the halter rope. He was starving hungry himself and still he had to take eggs across to the Wadges whose chickens weren't laying. He let the calf go into the paddock with the rest of the calf heifers and steers, thwacking with the rope to see it hump and shake its head. They were silly animals really.

Travelling at a slow jog, Albert reached the Wadge's white wood gate with not an egg cracked. He could see Alison Wadge's head, topped with the old green hat, pressed into Jessie's flank. She must have just begun because the milk hissing out hit the bottom of the pail like heavy rain.

'Hello Miss Wadge.'

She didn't pause which in one way was good as she was a real talker but also was a pity as it reduced his chances of getting invited for tea and cake.

'Here are the eggs, Miss Wadge,' said Albert. 'I'll put them in the kitchen will I?'

Miss Wadge nodded, 'And there's some cakes in there,' she was puffing and her bottom spread in every direction around the milking stool.

It seemed almost impossible that she had a living mother. Miss Alison Wadge was old herself; a shrivelled cowpea face. She had a tuft of white hair she sometimes coloured, with rosewater Matilda said, that made Albert think of the pink summer galahs. Old Mrs Wadge who was anchored for the rest of her life in a bed, had hardly any hair left. Albert had seen the skin below the struggling white strands and it was pale and flaking.

On Sundays after church the Ertles usually made a visit. They would take Alison Wadge home which made it such a squash Albert had to sit balancing on one of his sisters' knees and all of them were bony. Miss Wadge would go on through to the kitchen to make them the big pot of tea, leaving the Ertles to pay their respects to old Lil Wadge in her bedroom.

To approach the bed where she lay propped on pillows with peacocks embroidered in silk cottons, to put your hand into her blind creaking fingers, was frightening. She smelt of dying hair and the white paint on the bed peeled if you touched it. She kissed his sisters with spitty lips and bristles on her chin. The old sow, Albert would think, trying to work out whether the yellow bumps on that fleshy tongue were food or something worse. No cooking smells came through the sick, sour odours of lavender and urine. Once Albert peeked inside the commode. Pongy but someone always sat on it because with eight Ertles in the room there wasn't much choice. The gauze curtains of the front bedroom filtered the sun white and removed shadows. Albert would usually sit at the end of the bed where the plaid rug lay in neat folds, not listening to the murmuring voices his parents used and as far away as possible from the body that ended halfway down the bed clothes. If you sat too close, she poked her finger into your earwax and talked about growing pumpkin patches and potatoes.

Treading lightly so the floorboards wouldn't moan, Albert padded past the front bedroom with the eggs. The door was slightly ajar but he didn't bother stopping to take a peep inside. The kitchen smells billowing through the long hallway were rich and sweet.

Albert stuffed a patty cake into his mouth while his eyes adjusted to the dimmer light. It lay in two wide pans: stick jaw treacle toffee, golden and glossy and faintly marked in large squares. Ready to eat. Warm, with bubbles at the edges. Albert put a thick corner piece into his mouth and wrapped two bits in his hankie for later.

The toffee filled his mouth so that when he walked into the bathroom to collect another of Miss Wadge's lemon shaped soaps, that she ordered from Sydney and that Albert had been pinching whenever he got the chance, he could only yelp from between toffee stuck jaws. A mouth with no teeth groaned back. She was in the bath — old Lil Wadge, with nothing on at all.

Albert jerked his teeth open. The bottom front tooth he'd been loosening carefully for three weeks until it was just hanging, tore off with the toffee. He could taste the blood and his tongue touched the empty space. A human Lily. The purple and white breasts sagged and drowned like waterlogged pancakes. Albert backed through the door.

He arrived home panting to catch Christopher Wetherstone Clark's cat Boogler, snooping round in the thick, yellow scented shadows by the chookhouse. It was almost dinner time and Christopher Wetherstone Clark must have come round to pick up his Dad. They were standing near the dairy gate. Albert could see Monty scuffling the ground with his boots. The toffee in his mouth was a small, vinegar-sweet circle on his tongue and he sqwarked like a galah to get their attention. They waved. Albert began to hop towards them, left leg bent, right foot springing the ground as the fence posts leaned at angles and shivered in camphor-laurel shade. In his back pocket, the toffees, tooth and two perfectly shaped lemon soaps, bumped and joggled together.

Curly Wig the Nob

'By the cripes almighty you're a slow poke Al,' Christopher Wetherstone Clark's hands danced in the air with impatience and cold. It was early but not early enough for Christopher Wetherstone Clark who Albert said must never sleep a wink.

'I'm coming,' Albert emerged struggling out of the shed with a pointy looking sack of gear and his pig dog Beetle.

'Don't tell me you're bringing Beetle! You can't bring him Albert. He'll never make it.'

Albert set Beetle on the ground. 'Why shouldn't he. Made it last year, didn't he. Only stiff cause he's cold. Anyway, Adelaine's fixed something up for him.'

'Oh no Albert. You're not going to dress him in those.'

'Can't see why not,' Albert began to manoeuvre Beetle into an old flannel vest of his Dad's. 'She's fixed them perfectly. They won't fall off and Beetle will be warm. Won't you Beetle? So what's wrong with that?'

'He won't be able to go to the toilet, that's what.'

'Adelaine's not stupid you know. She thought of that. And there's a hole for his tail. Now you're right, aren't you Beetle?'

Beetle thumped his bald, four times fractured tail in an attempt at real enthusiasm. He was eleven years old. Almost ninety, Albert told everyone, if you converted that into human years. Albert's mother had a photo she kept on her dressing table of Albert with a toothy smile, holding Beetle as a tiny pup. Even Beetle was smiling.

Beetle had only just begun to be an embarrassment. Miss Aimsley had asked Albert to stop bringing him to school. She said it was because of fleas. In fact the reason was because Beetle had lost control of his donger. He would sit in the sun with it poking out. Then he'd go to sleep and then it wouldn't be red or shiny anymore. And it was awful for Beetle and Miss Aimsley as well, the day it wouldn't go in by itself. Miss Aimsley had lent Albert a jar of vaseline to assist its retreat. Everyone had watched: grit got in. All the girls laughed and Miss Aimsley went white about the nose and said soon afterwards that Beetle mustn't come to school anymore. Fleas she said, but there were fleas in the sand and only on Monday a flea had hopped from Albert's hair onto his sums book. Christopher Wetherstone Clark had laughed and trapped it in a ball of ear wax.

It was because of Beetle's gammy hip that his tail was so broken. Beetle loved to be around when the horses hooves were rasped. Most dogs like to chew on a bit of hoof and Beetle did too, only he liked to lie underneath the horse when he was doing it. Now his hip had packed it in he wasn't fast enough to move out of the way when the horses moved. Still, Albert persisted in including him in his favourite old activities. As there was nothing Beetle liked better than to come on fishing and kite flying days, there was no way he was being left behind, whatever Christopher Wetherstone Clark thought.

'Come on Beetle,' said Albert.

'Come on then Beetle,' Christopher Wetherstone Clark prodded him up with his boot. 'Looks like you're coming.'

'Eh Beetle,' Albert gave him a pat of encouragement and they were off.

The frost was so thick it crunched like ice beneath their feet. Half a moon lay in the sky fading lighter and lighter in layers of green. Albert hoped the clover wouldn't get burnt. It felt cold enough for it. They crossed the edge of the lucerne paddock and the white cover of frost was silent and complete. From a clump of trees further across, the cattle moved thin and ghostly towards the fence.

Christopher snorted white steam from his mouth. 'You know Jason Granger thinks we're nutters getting up early like this.'

Albert thought his friend an idiot for bothering to tell Jason Granger what they were up to. 'So when did you ever care what Wopper Granger has to say? Want a tongue cutter?' Albert offered a twisted bag of acid balls. 'He's probably still chained to his bed. With nothing on. That's what his mother does to them if they play up.'

'Yeah, all the Granger kids are queer looking,' said Christopher. 'It's their haircuts I think. Makes them mad. Their mother shears them every month with mane clippers.'

'I heard her doing it once,' Albert said. 'They were all crying. Like plovers, even Jason. She'd made him bald just about,' he crunched an acid ball.

Christopher Wetherstone Clark laughed. 'Not that you can talk about haircuts Al, you Curly Wig the Nob.'

'That's a really funny baby that Granger one,' Albert said but Christopher Wetherstone Clark had outstripped him climbing the hill and was out of hearing. The sun was warming things up at last except Beetle's tongue grew so heavy with slobber Albert was afraid he'd tread on it. He heaved Beetle onto his hip. 'Come on you old woop. It's not that bad,' Albert scratched Beetle's ear and gave up trying to catch Christopher. He walked too fast with those long legs of his.

Jason Granger's baby sister was stranger even than Sidney had been. Quieter. Sitting in the dirt with not a stitch on and hair that peaked out like feathers on a seedy, wobbling bird straight out of the shell. The only Granger yet to escape its mother's scissors.

Jason reckoned that the first noises to come out of his little sister's mouth had been a sigh, then a soft *oh dear* and a softer sigh still. It was all she said so far. She could also make a pffing sound with her lips. The mother made the same sound when her hands were full and she couldn't flick the hair from her eyes. But the baby did it because the mother did it. A baby echo.

Christopher Wetherstone Clark called them the Family of Sighers.

Albert was puffed when he caught up to Christopher Wetherstone Clark. Beetle had slobbered Albert's shirt wet and he had to admit Beetle ponged. Of old hair, of old pee, of old flea dirt, of old dog . . . old was old and you could smell it whatever its disguise.

These tunnels they had to crawl through were quite old. Lantana tunnels full of dry yellow silence. If you stopped crawling it was as if the world stopped too. They'd ploughed their way through them last winter but already the bushes were overgrowing and mysterious.

Christopher Wetherstone Clark stopped at the first rock overhang. There were red berried weeds and Cape Gooseberries where there hadn't been before. Spider webs too, with spiders in hiding. They both had rock collections with the digging stones they'd found here in these semi caves. Cocoons of half dark. They'd cleaned the caves out of small, moon shaped stones with edges, that even now could slice a finger and that Christopher Wetherstone Clark once used to skin a mouse.

They paused for a moment. Airless and quiet except for Beetle panting.

'Might as well keep going, eh what Al?'

'Yep,' too much to crawl inside. Emptied spaces. Not even proper caves.

It became difficult to move through the growth. Albert thought of all Christopher Wetherstone Clark's words: clobber bum, poofystinkles, slobber gobalob, flapdoodle, bosh and bunkum.

'Shittyfatteners,' they groaned the word together, seeing at the same time the tangled bush ahead. Which made them laugh. Pommy words were funny but good to say.

26

They ate lunch at the top, pleased because already a wind was blowing. Albert fed most of his crusts to Beetle because Albert was riding two of Pimmy Rankin's horses in the Picnic races coming up and also because he secretly wondered whether crusts were responsible after all for the state of his hair, which just lately seemed more curly than ever before.

Tucking Beetle in first underneath the sack, Albert picked up the kites. They were Christopher Wetherstone Clark's latest design; slender and small and Albert wondered if they'd ever get them in the air, let alone fly them. Spread across the frames was some of the flax fibre from New Zealand that Albert had nicked from Tindley the saddler. They were scrap bits that Albert was sure Mr Tindley wouldn't have missed anyway. And as his Mum was always saying, what the eye can't see, the mind cannot grieve over.

For string that was long enough and lighter than fishing line, Albert had some of his sister's embroidery cottons. Crimson and green.

The kites flew. Almost like birds thought Albert, so high you could barely see them. He watched Christopher Wetherstone Clark along the slope of the hill, his shadow racing before him and Beetle trailing behind, excited and stiff. Albert preferred less movement. Letting the kite turn and swoop by itself — the tug of the cotton on the controlling finger.

They flew them into the afternoon light until their kite strings twisted and wove together, crimson and green, refusing to sail apart and dive bombing finally into the branches of a whipple tree.

'Bloody hell,' said Albert.

'Shitty bloody fattener,' said Christopher Wetherstone Clark, watching the kites as they ripped.

'They've had it,' said Albert.

'We could try and get them.' Christopher Wetherstone Clark began to walk for the tree.

'They'd be no good.'

'Who says?'

'Me.'

'Don't be such a stinker Al.'

Albert waited at the bottom of the tree while Christopher tried to shin up the smooth bulging bark.

'Come back. Cripeys, you idiot. They're too far out. You'd have to be an acrobat.' Albert threw his voice like a net but Christopher Wetherstone Clark was already moving along the first forked branch. Albert stopped looking up, his neck sore. There were ants in Christopher Wetherstone Clark's socks and in the glossy sap oozing from knobs in the tree.

'Hey!' yelled Christopher Wetherstone Clark. He was standing on the main trunk and holding onto the branch above him. 'Hey Al, I can see someone coming.'

'Like hell you can. Give up.'

'Hey, it's Jason Granger.'

It was Jason Granger. Christopher Wetherstone Clark abandoned the kites. 'He's got the gar rod Albert!'

As if it were some sort of feat to carry a piece of bamboo, to drag a gar rod behind you when there wasn't nearly enough water in the creek for gar. Albert sat on a rock by himself in the gully, scratching Beetle where he liked to be scratched, watching the other two fool around in the water. No way there'd be any fish within miles now. Beetle licked Albert's feet and between his toes where it tickled. Albert felt his throat was all jammed up — like he'd eaten too many hard boiled egg sandwiches.

They had both stripped off but still hadn't got right into the water. They were splashing at each other and screaming just like girls would do. Christopher Wetherstone Clark was white and bony, the Pom. Jason's body was browner and longer like a moth cocoon.

'Come on in Curly Wig the Nob,' one of them yelled. Their voices were high and excited. Albert closed his eyes. Christopher Wetherstone Clark was a real goop.

Once Albert had come here by himself. After a flood

and the creek so full it was impossible to see the fence that normally crossed the water. That day there'd been a man with a girl. He was stroking a leafy twig across her stomach. Albert had thought of spiders or stinging grubs and stayed watching for the yell that never came. The fence was still there — leaning towards the water, growing moss and hairy with dead river weed. It was hard to know who owned the land. Come the next heavy rain and the fence would be gone anyway.

A few striped stocking mozzies were hanging around and Albert squashed them on his leg. His fingers were pulling seconds from dandelion clocks he caught drifting by in the wind. There was no point getting out the handline but there were minnows in the little pool near Albert's rock. From his pocket he took a big nappy pin and pierced a ball of bread onto the tip. He rolled the bread ball into mashed mosquito for flavour and then waited for the transparent fish and caught them too, while Beetle heaved and snorted asleep. Albert would sell the minnows to Christopher Wetherstone Clark for Boogler the cat, no discounts given.

Competitions of Pain

Every day after school they would have Competitions of Pain. They were Jason's idea. He invented all the stages and intricacies of the games and he always won. First it was just a matter of sticking burning matches into the heel of the foot, where the skin was so tough nothing could be felt. That was as easy as poking a stick into clay. Except Jason made little Pod Mitty do it too. Little Pod who was never allowed by his Mum to go barefoot. He screamed when Jason held him down and jammed a match into the pink skin under his toes. Ever since Jason's little sister had caught the measles and died, he was meaner and more cunning with his competitions. Everyone in school got the measles, even Sidney who'd had them already as a five year old.

It had been a quiet funeral. Nobody much crying but for Jason who was still a bit spotty himself. He cried so much that in the end it wasn't possible to see what were the measles and what were red blotches. Embarrassing and Jason not bothering to do anything about his runny nose — just letting it snivel down his shirt. Albert had been glad enough to have CWC there on the other side until he'd started crying too. Albert had stiffened in his pew, sitting straight on his bottom bones, his hand half way to his pocket, reaching for a snot rag to give Jason. Not hearing the minister's words of consolation, only the snuffling of his two friends either side of him. It was impossible that this could happen.

Then, unbelievably, as the service ended and Jason's Dad picked up the coffin, Albert too had begun to cry; in strange sounds as the small box went by, light enough for one to carry. The Ertles' wreath of daisies Albert had watched Jinnie and Eva and his mother make the night before, slipped off at the back so that poor Mr Granger had to stoop right there in the aisle, with the coffin under one arm and pick it up. When that happened, Albert was sure he could hear the body inside hitting the end with a soft thump and he hoped Jason hadn't heard because it was a sad and dreadful sound.

The organ droned a funeral hymn and everyone trailed out. Only the Grangers were to go to the small hole on the edge of the cemetery, that everyone had seen, newly dug, on their way to church: the fresh dirt, the clover disturbed. Albert thought he would stop jumping gravestones on his horse.

Back at school they said nothing about their first funeral. But as it turned out, September was a month of death and strange coincidences and every afternoon, Competitions of Pain. Jason organised them for the lunch hour. Usually there were ten competitors, which delighted Jason. It meant they could divide into two teams and it was better that way.

CWC was always in on them. He was trying to grow a beard but the hair simply wasn't there. A thick cluster of pimples grew between his eyebrows. If Albert happened to call him Christopher Wetherstone Clark, he'd call Albert a pain in the bum. The three letter abbreviation of CWC had been an idea of Jason's:

See Double You See

W.C.

Water Closet

Wetherstone Clark

Wetherstone Christopher.

Jason liked to play games with words and was there when Monty, CWC's Dad, had purchased two water closets at the Wadges' Clearance Sale. Once old Mrs Wadge had died, Alison Wadge was quick to sell up and move away to the city. Albert's Dad picked up a few good milkers very cheap. Lots of people turned up for the sale and everything was sold — right down to the patterned cake tins all the Ertle children had dipped their hands into so often. Bottles of pickles and marmalade with rusty lids were snapped up. Alison Wadge had a reputation as a good cook and her jams always won prizes at the annual show. Christopher Wetherstone Clark's mother got the egg cups with the blue stripes on white. There were three mattresses with yellow stains and an oak dresser that at first no one would make a starting bid on. Jacky Toll, the perspiring auctioneer, ran the show, throwing in a couple of mozzie nets with mildew corners, to encourage the bids on bed linen.

After Miss Aimsley married, there was a new teacher at school. Miss Hossy. Miss Hannah Hossy. She even had a face like a horse; a long carthorse nose and hair growing up on her high cheekbones. She arrived in a bad month. Jason Granger took an instant dislike to her and never stopped doing things to annoy her. Like chiselling an entire ball bearing game into the wood of his desk, so that the whole desk had to be picked up and tilted to play. Everyone took to drawing pictures of her while she tried to read aloud. With tears in her voice she'd walk around the room and say that no one had made the nose long enough. Sometimes she used a whippy piece of cane to punish with. There were ridges along it that broke the flesh on legs. And that was all part of Jason's new game. Seeing how much pain he could take.

Out of school Albert didn't see so much of his old friends now he and Sidney were having to help with the milking. Albert's Dad said they were not much of a substitute for Monty who had known everything there was to know about dairy cows.

Albert wondered what would happen without Monty if this Spring one of the cows got bloat. Last year one of his Dad's best Jersey crosses raided the lucerne. Monty knew what to do: a warm drench with turpentine and treacle mash with a sizeable helping of whiskey to boot.

When this didn't work he made Mrs Ertle run for a carving knife. He knew exactly where to stick it in so the rumen would puncture — a point on the left side between the hips and last rib where the slight depression was. The fermented air rushed out through the bit of pipe Monty had inserted and the cow was as right as rain. Albert thought that if he was by himself with a bloating beast he wouldn't do a good job. Not without messing something up. Difficult enough trying to milk ten cattle within the space of an hour. Monty had been the expert there too. Just Monty and Dad could finish off the herd of forty in less than two hours. It was all in the way you used your fingers and shoulders Monty told him. 'No good simply pulling,' he'd say. 'You've got to develop your own rhythm.' Albert had milked since he was seven but never could speed up. Monty said he should be glad he didn't have to do it in England, in Kent, where it was so cold you couldn't move your fingers and the cow's udders grew such long hair it had to be singed off with a burning taper and then the teats rubbed with lard to stop cracking and sores. Monty knew so many things about saltpetre solutions, mashes, the correct usages of Stockholm Tar — how to fix milk fever with no more than cold water, the whites of eggs and a mustard-turpentine blister applied to the cow's back. It was a pity Monty left. It meant Albert had to start regular milking. Up until then he'd only had to on Monty's days off.

Jason and CWC and some of the other townies were talking about leaving school and getting jobs. CWC said he was going to try at the Buttery and Creamery. A depressing thought: Christopher Wetherstone Clark smelling dull and cheesy after working butter in unheated rooms, old milk under his fingernails, his whole life ruled by oily lumps floating round in butter milk. Albert knew all about it because Adelaine worked there before she was married. You went mouldy alongside old cheese. It was beyond contemplation. Jason said he was going to Sydney as soon as he could. His uncle on the Railways could get him a job. CWC said there were lots of perks at the Buttery and Creamery — free condensed milk and butter at a discount.

All this talk of departures left Albert feeling vague and nervy. It made his skin tingle. He'd never given the matter much thought. There was the farm and he'd taken out a jockey apprenticeship of kinds with Pimmy Rankin's Stables. In a couple of years he could be riding at tracks all over the place.

Anything would have to be better than the Buttery. Even the Sugar Mill. Or you could head west and get any sort of work. There were always local jobs to be found stirring molasses at the mill. Or fencing and carrying. No one said you had to stay put in the same town. And what of Boogler? Cats weren't allowed near dairy factories. It said so in the Act. Surely Christopher Wetherstone Clark wouldn't abandon his cat. Adelaine said a cat with kittens found in one of the Buttery store rooms was drowned. And all the kittens. Before anyone could get a chance to say they'd take them, they were all put into a weighted sack and into the river they went.

Boogler's death happened unexpectedly. CWC said it was Boogler's hormones taking control over him that led to his downfall. He was found dead with a squashed in skull the same day Beetle died. Something had got Boogler though no one could say exactly what.

As Boogler's revived virility took him on journeys away from CWC, white tipped tail pointed to the sky, Beetle aged suddenly and Albert couldn't take him anywhere ever again. Beetle's hair turned white around his ears and flanks. He fell down trying to lift his leg and had to squat. His ears wept an evil smelling wax, blocking out all sounds.

Beetle died in the slatted lines of light under the verandah. Sidney, who'd been sitting above with the weekend comics and dropping flakes of cold gramma pie onto Beetle to try and perk him up, swore he saw

Beetle's tail wag just before he snored his last snore.

'A peaceful end Al,' Sidney tried to reassure his big brother who seemed morose rather than saddened by the event. It made Sidney wish he'd been more elaborate in describing the incredible cacophony of sounds that accompanied that last snore — the popping wheezes and whistles from both ends.

Swallo MacLernon and Jason hovered while CWC and Albert dug the ground. Jason laughed. Laughed at Beetle being dead. Laughed because his legs wouldn't bend to fit the hole. Thought it a good joke that both CWC's and Al's strange animals had kicked the bucket on the same day. Said they were soft for knocking teeth out of Boogler and Beetle to keep. Said they shouldn't have put a flame tree over the graves because the roots would twist through the ribs and eye sockets and bust them into pieces.

'Just shut it Granger,' Albert said, tamping the dirt.

'Don't be such a touchy bastard Al. Isn't he a touchy bastard? It's only a bloody dog and cat you've buried.' Jason appealed to Christopher Wetherstone Clark and Swallo for support. 'Come on, we'll see you later Albert-a Buried-a-Beetle.'

And Christopher Wetherstone Clark, the stupid nong, went with them.

After that, nothing was the same. It was like Albert's and Christopher Wetherstone Clark's friendship had been buried alongside Beetle and Boogler; had been ruptured by some intricate root system of betrayal and allegiance.

There was a week of rain and Albert thought he'd go mad at night with the water plopping into the pails, thoughts going bad inside his head. Everywhere a smell of mildew and damp.

He thought of the rain in the soil and how Beetle and Boogler without coffins were looking. Army worms invaded the vegetable patch and he thought about those too. In the dairy, the cattle slithered and were unsteady in the green smelling mud. The paddocks looked like the smeared efforts of a child finger painter, with no borders except for the weatherboard of window frames. Poke your fingers into bored eyes and the world went crooked. Signposts pointed down. There were no directions to go by. Marshmallow weed and Crofton went wild and smothered known landmarks. The whole world limped along under storm and drizzle, with the last of the mandarins and oranges dropping to rot in the mud. Everything a smudged mess, and Pimmy's horses still to be ridden, stables to be mucked out.

People wondered if the river would flood. Sidney read comics and abandoned homework. Mrs Ertle's bulbs lost their colour. Jinnie said she couldn't wait to be married and played old songs over and over on the pianola that made Albert's teeth squeak. *Ragamuffin Romeo, Meander in the Meadow* and *Goodnight Irene goodnight I'll see you in my dreams.*

There was no word from Matilda who was training in Sydney as a teacher for the Department of Public Instruction. Eva and Rebecca learnt how to bake a fruitcake and sat up giggling late into the night waiting for it to cook in the middle. Jinnie did one hundred feet of finger knitting and ran out of red wool. Albert made her cry by unravelling it and telling her to start again. After losing his forty seventh bout of noughts and crosses, Sidney said he hated the pizzling rain and was walloped round the ears for swearing.

The leather of unused school shoes covered in a white fungus. Work boots ponged too, rotting from the inside and Albert's Mum found maggots growing in the wet clothes and had to boil them all over again. His Dad tried to be funny, dropping his teeth into his tea and pretending surprise to see them there. Sitting at the table for meals, Albert listened to the rain and to noises of eating: chewing, swallowing, spit rushing down his father's throat and rushing back up to cope with unexpected lumps of gristle.

36

To fill time, Albert read the In Memorium notices in yellow newspapers. The words about deepening shadows and of endless toil and of distances too far to travel, gave Albert a feeling of unspeakable gloom. His mouth filled with the metallic taste of despair and longing. It was like sucking on a halfpenny that had passed through a hundred hands. There was something sad and painful in reading about gentle eyes that would weep no more, lambs Jesus had called home, memories locked in hearts with golden, crystal and precious keys, silent tears, the silver gates of memory: reading the same verses over for Wiggins, Joyces, Smiths and Pierces.

Albert thought his head would crack like an egg if Sidney read out one more cartoon to him using his special cartoon voices.

At night he made his bed damper using one hand under the sheets and only half trying to aim the globby jets onto bits of folded newspaper. He dreamt of watery worlds, the feel of swaying weeds on his body, of algae growing on his feet. In the mornings his toes sweated. He ate too much of the dark fruit cake with the doughy middle and made smells worse than Beetle but no Beetle to blame them on. Fleas invaded the kitchen floor.

The one good thing about the rain was it called a halt to school and Jason's after school activities. No more Competitions of Pain whilst the rain lasted.

Seeing if you could beat Jason's time of 21 seconds holding a magnifying glass in the sun over your belly button.

Eating the purple and white fruit of thistles with only a minute to peel away the thorns. Little Pod Mitty hadn't been able to talk or eat for a week afterwards, his tongue and mouth were so swollen.

Sewing the tips of your fingers together with a stolen needle and thread.

Tramping bare foot on nettles and not being allowed to use the juices of the fleshy dock leaves to ease the stinging. Not meant to use spit even.

Pull ups from a tree branch till your muscles felt like splitting apart and your head throbbed.

Going without shoes in the muddy part of the river where people were known to have been stung by deadly Bullrouts.

Jason Granger had turned as mean as a sour mare in season. No doubt about that. What Albert couldn't understand was why anyone bothered with him at all.

One morning, eight days after the rain began, the clouds curdled and broke up and Albert woke to see sun in the leaves of the camphorlaurel through the verandah louvres. He lay watching the clouds behind the tree, not convinced by their fading bruise colour next to clear sky. To have a better look, he climbed out of his crumpled sheets. Just as he thought, there was more rain coming. He rummaged around the bottom of his bed for his left sock that must have come off in the night. While the break in the weather lasted he decided he was going to see CWC.

Albert passed his Dad finishing the morning milking and yelled he'd be back in plenty of time to give a hand later. He booted Ned into a canter, slapping the reins either side to get a bit of life into the old fellow. There was no chance of old Ned being stupid after a week with no work. Albert kicked his muddy sides a bit harder and perched his knees up as if in a racing pad. He tried to make Ned arch his neck, thinking hard of something smart to say and nearly falling off when Ned shied at a puddle. Maybe Mrs Wetherstone Clark would have some breakfast left over. Cold toad-in-the-hole from the night before would go down well.

It was his lucky day. Mrs Wetherstone Clark was dishing up fried eggs to Monty when he arrived and toast done in the fat from the pan. A dish of toad-in-the-hole steamed next to a slab of yellow butter. Albert's mouth watered.

'Thanks all the same,' said Albert, knocking back an

offer of thick gravy to go with his breakfast, 'This'll be fine thanks.' He chewed his dough covered sausages quickly on his way to CWC's bedroom. The first mouthful was always the best. That feeling of grease and salty meat slipping down never disappointed. Albert thought it a pity his own Mum didn't hold with going to the fuss of battering her sausages. His mother always could shut him up by saying he'd grow too heavy for Pimmy's horses if he ate like that every day. Since Mrs Wetherstone Clark was an enormous size, Albert couldn't argue. As fat and comforting as the roly poly puddings with lashings of treacle she cooked.

CWC was a grey lump under his blankets. The bedroom was full of mouse skins stretched out on frames of pegs to dry.

'Oy, what's going on here?'

Christopher Wetherstone Clark grunted and pulled his head out. 'I'm tanning them,' he waved at a jar of liquid by the foot of the bed. 'Made it up myself. It's my own mix. Jace's idea really. You do it with wattle bark. Scrape it off with a knife and boil it up. Working already. It's really good.'

'Where did all the mice come from?' Albert asked.

'Had an invasion now Booglers gone. Had to set the traps. Had to do something in the rain. What've you been up to?'

'But what are you going to do with them?' Albert could hardly believe the number of mice pelts. Suspended from the curtain rail was another line of grey skins.

'Don't know really. Thought you might come up with something bright.'

'Well don't look at me. You're mad. They're not big enough for anything. You should have done something a decent size.'

'We did,' Christopher Wetherstone Clark pulled from under his bed a bigger frame. The tortoise-shell coat of Boogler was going well, hardly affected at all by its brief

39

stay underground. 'We went back and got him afterwards. Could have got Beetle too but he didn't have much hair left in the end. Y'know, the mange.'

Albert bent closer to the skin. It was smeared with salt. 'You're really disgusting. You know that. It's sick. You sliced him up. You chopped Boogler open.'

'He was dead Albert. Made a mess though doing his head. Had to abandon it.'

'What about the tree we put in?'

'Oh, it'll be alright. Jason did a good job putting it back.'

'What did you do with, you know, the remains?' Albert had an awful thought of Boogler without skin. Not smooth and fluid and well proportioned but hacked by knives and smelling of raw and gouged meat.

'We put that back. Back with Beetle.'

'Yeah Al, we put him back,' Jason walked into the room eating toast. 'Not bad are they?' Jason unpinned one of the mouse skins for Albert to feel.

Albert looked at the small piece of fur in his hands. The skin was turning to a soft, pale leather. 'They're alright,' said Albert. 'What are you two doing today?'

'We got anything planned yet Water Closet?' Jason winked slyly at Christopher Wetherstone Clark.

'I'm having breakfast first,' said Christopher Wetherstone Clark and headed through the door in his pyjamas.

'You can come if you want Albert, if you're game that is,' Jason grinned. 'There'll be a few others along I expect.' Jason picked up the jar of tanning fluid and began to paint the underside of Boogler with a badly chewed toothbrush. 'Thought for a while this rain would muck everything up. Humidity and all that. But only one of the mouse skins went rotten in one corner. Isn't that right CWC and that was because we didn't get all the meat off.'

Albert wondered what Jason was up to now, what was planned, what horrible competition he'd invented while the rain hammered the town's tin rooves. There was a strange smell in the room. Of wattle bark and dead things and silk worms in a shoe box on the window sill. Albert opened them up for a look. They were white and fat, the cocoons of most of them already spun. In fact only one caterpillar to be seen in amongst the mulberry leaves. In no time at all they would eat their way out as velvety cream moths, mate, lay eggs, grow tatty, die flapping into the ground before summer arrived.

Jason walked over and picked up a cocoon. He began to wind the thread onto a matchstick already covered in silk. 'Going to come then Albert?'

'Come where?'

'To where we're going.'

Albert wished he'd stopped at home to take Sid and his muscovy ducks sailing in the big troughs that would be overflowing now with clean rain water. 'Guess so,' said Albert. There was no alternative he could think of. 'I'm going to get another sausage,' he said.

Albert walked into the kitchen. Mrs Wetherstone Clark was laughing hard at something Monty had said, her lips greasy and smiling, when she took her stroke.

She took a stroke. Albert had heard his mother say it before. Had heard the words and the more grisly details being exchanged above his head in the days when he was small enough for his mother to take him shopping, and stopped to talk in the street. It was different altogether seeing one — terrible to see her body heave and sway on top of the small kitchen chair. Monty gripped her by the elbow, was thumping her back. Was he hoping it was just a bit of toad-in-the-hole stuck in her windpipe? She slumped off the chair, overtoppled. Landed on the floor like a dying cow. Out of the corner of his eye, Albert saw the Wetherstone Clark's nanny goat eating his horse Ned's tail. He had an urge to wave his arms and shout. Christopher Wetherstone Clark wasn't doing anything much and Monty was stretching her out, putting tea towels under her head, loosening her apron. She wasn't coughing anymore, her hands twitched. Her skin was massing in clouds of purple and red.

Monty kept beating her back. Stuff came dribbling out — small particles of meat, morsels of yellow egg but nothing large. No big sausage lumps. She wasn't breathing. Albert saw that, saw her legs poking out, turning blue, blotching over.

She lay on the cold kitchen floor, a huge human mound, arms spread like a crucifix. Christopher Wetherstone Clark's sausage fell from his hand and lay beside her fox coloured eyes that were dulling and popping. Mrs Clark's birthday present, a new kettle CWC had saved like anything for, whistled from the wood stove. There was a smell of burnt toast shrivelling up next to the kettle.

Bad luck runs in sets of four, not three like the old saying said. Albert trailed home from his fourth burial of the month and knew this to be true. He wasn't going to the cake and sandwiches being held. In Mrs Wetherstone Clark's kitchen and all. It was still raining alright, the river flooded and school shut for another week at least.

Bacon rind had caused the choking, not a stroke. Albert hoped they hadn't cut open that laughing throat.

When he arrived home, Albert picked up his boxful of four leafed clovers, carefully saved and dried over two years and the biggest collection anyone had ever heard of. Two hundred and four all up. Albert always ate one before a race. Just a mutant seed producing the extra leaf, his Dad told him. But Albert had always believed he was lucky, that he found so many four leafed clovers because he was extra lucky.

Now he took his box of four leafed clovers and tipped them into the mud. They wrinkled the puddles — made patterns with the rain coming down.

Adelaine's Child

The knitting needles lay pointed in the shape of an open compass to the empty chair. Caught by evening wind the thin paper pattern fell on the floor. The baby jumper was gone. Its absence left the dark room with no colour. Each night of the week he'd stayed, his mother knitted: a green and tiny jumper ready for Jinnie's first baby whether it was a boy or a girl. He was Uncle Albert five times over now and back in the nick of time, everyone said, for the double Christening. He'd brought home two Christening mugs, hallmarked in England, with racehorses and crouching jockeys engraved in fine lines. Already he'd decided to leave them either end of the mantlepiece before leaving. They were hidden under the bed, wrapped in two shirts. He tried to forget how originally they were meant for Adelaine's twins. He didn't send them though, not after the youngest one died.

He'd missed so many events, births, funerals, marriages. In his wallet he carried all the small yellowing oblongs of newspaper announcements his mother posted. He tried to think of the last family occasion he was at but unless it was his own farewell, everyone sneezing yellow wattle and crying, he couldn't remember. Everything was too long ago. Most recently he'd missed his father's funeral by five months and Jinnie's wedding by twelve and a half weeks. Whole slabs of rituals like appointments he'd failed to keep but could never make again. He felt his absences made him a stranger. But he couldn't stay for these Christenings, or Jinnie's baby still weeks away, or Matilda's proposed visit.

His mother was quieter. Albert missed her old loud voice. She was forever appearing unexpectedly around corners where she'd been doing nothing — just wandered the garden and house in gumboots or slippers. She didn't seem to care which, Adelaine told Albert. A Creeping Jesus, she said.

It used to be their mother's favourite expression if Sidney or any one of them was mooning round with a runny nose.

From his old verandah bed, in the same position under the long windows, he was neither inside nor outside the house. He could watch both worlds. On the second night after his arrival, he heard the soft clack of needles begin and from his bed could look through the windows into the mirror of the oak corner cabinet. He could see his mother's reflections distorted by angles, knitting crookedly in all the faded afternoons. Her right fingers had permanently locked sideways with arthritis, which made each stitch more difficult.

In under over off.
In over under off.
In under over on.

She recited stitch sequence like verse, or chanted — suddenly quiet when checking the emerging shape. Then knitting steadily, silent except for the needles clicking and the unravellings of wool in her lap. He heard these softer noises beneath the clatter from somebody in the kitchen and the sounds of night from outside the louvred verandah.

It worried him to see her stomach fallen onto her legs like an old woman, a comfortable arm rest as she worked.

'She's knitting her sadness,' whispered the silent daughter of Adelaine, who'd crept into the other end of his bed. He could smell her sweaty child feet.

'Knitting her sadness,' she said again. And Albert thought he could see how each stitch was a knot of something lost.

'I'm Adelaine's child,' she answered when he asked

44

to be reminded of her name. The names of all his child relations, the pet family names of each, confused him. He'd forgotten Adelaine was still in the house tidying up.

'I'm allowed to cook a cake 'cause you're back. I was a twin once,' she disappeared, crawling up through the bed, untucking the edges so she'd be next to his dislocated shoulder. His thin chest was strapped round with beige bandages soaked in warm water so they would shrink tighter during the night.

'Is it hurting?'

Albert watched his mother through the glassy reflections and felt afraid to speak.

'You can see better,' she talked to his ear, 'if you kneel. It's the knitting room not the sitting room.' The bed bent in the middle. They knelt together. The tall, thin windows caught his own image and he saw how tight and hungry his face had become. Altogether the three figures were like a painting: the old lady knitting into her own darkness, the returned son and in the lower right corner of the shifting picture, the pink cheeked girl in pigtails. Albert thought she must be a hair-sucker because each pigtail had stiffened dry into pointy tips.

'I once had a broken toe,' she'd lost interest in her grandmother who hadn't once looked up. Full of admiration she fingered her Uncle Albert's bandage. 'Tell me again how it happened?'

'An unlucky fall,' said Albert. 'Muddy track. Two horses in front fell. It happens.'

When she left the bed it was cold and draughty near his toes where the blankets and sheets were loose. There was the uncomfortable feel of biscuit crumbs, buttery and sharp under his back. She'd looked like Wee Willie Winkie in her striped wool stockings as she hurried to her mother's voice. Wee Willie Winkie running through the night.

But tonight no one was with him and his mother wasn't knitting. From the bed he looked again through the windows into the room. All the children had been again. Their awkward affection made him muddle the names more. He was clumsy with his shoulder and the babies. His pinched jockey hips were so bony they made the littlies cry when he picked them up for a better look.

Albert left his bed to make himself some tea. The kitchen teapot was nowhere to be found so he went slowly into the sitting room. The silver pot was tarnishing inside the cabinet. There was the acid smell of emptiness. Sulphuric. No tea had warmed the pot for a long time and some one had tried to scrape the deep brown tannin from the bottom. The silver shone through like scratchmarks.

He tried to remember his mother as she must have been but her outline was vague and always confined by the doorways of the weeping green weatherboard house. Now she wore shawls of fine wool over cotton dresses, as if she was forever chilled. The shawls had holes like leaf skeletons, the flesh shrivelled away, leaving the fragile tapering frame. When he'd first hugged her, his shoulder a sharp pain, her arms through the lacework startled him. Her muscles were gone.

The jumper was lying in the folds of the baggy armchair that had been his father's. The knitting was in pieces, waiting to be sewn together. The edges curled. A jar of biscuits was on the table next to a rimless pair of spectacles. He couldn't help unscrewing the lid to smell the rich butter, or resist digging with calloused fingers and eating four biscuits one after the other. The sugar crunched between his brown teeth used to black shag tobacco, not sweetness. More slowly, he chewed down another two. The darkness, the shape of the old round room, protected him; hid the activity of his jaw. Adelaine's child must have been curled up in the darkest corner. 'Don't finish all of them,' her voice was indignant. 'I'll get all the blame.' She climbed down from a chair and went over to the biscuits. 'You're only meant to have one with milk,' the tilt of her face accused. He felt he'd betrayed some other forgotton rite.

Albert rubbed his fingers — they were greasy, sweet, guilty. He offered her the half-eaten seventh biscuit. But she was forgiving him already. 'S'all right really. You have it. I'll get my own if you get me a glass of milk.'

When he came back she was eating by the window. Her mouth chewed like some delicate stick insect. She put a warm, sticky hand conspiratorially on his leg. A baby was crying somewhere else in the house. They could hear the soothing hush of voices.

'Can you show me your belly when you eat a biscuit,' she asked slyly.

'Why do you want to see that?'

''Cause Scully thinks 'cause you're a jockey you can see the food going down.'

Albert looked at her expectant face. If he waited any longer, he saw she'd run away. So he took the bit of biscuit she held up and lifted his shirt. His stomach was round and tight already from the forbidden biscuits he'd eaten. She could almost see the shape of them sitting in there.

He swallowed the biscuit and almost choked. It was worth it though for her laugh. She giggled, then laughed and laughed to see the face he pulled, his skinny chest, ribs like the racehorses he rode. As well, she was laughing at herself for believing her cousin who said you could see the food under their Uncle Albert's skin.

Albert let his shirt fall, wondering how to get rid of the extra weight before Saturday's races.

'The bicky jar's almost empty, Uncle Albert,' she pushed her hand into his. 'You'll tell Gramma it wasn't me?'

'I'll tell her. Don't you think about it.'

'Thankyou Uncle Albert. Scully wouldn't . . .' Adelaine began to call from outside. 'That's Mum. I'd better go and say goodbye to Gramma. You're my best Uncle,' she turned uncertainly at the door. 'I'll see you on Sunday? At the Christenings?' As if she almost knew she wouldn't.

Albert returned to the kitchen for a dose of hot choko chutney so he'd vomit. He ate four big spoonfuls. The ponderous black marble clock, a trophy from child-hood, tocked away the minutes. He drank warm water and felt his stomach abused and bloating. The drip stained porcelain sink, the choko on the edges of the jar were a soiled and despairing colour.

'Our teacher snoogles on the unwindy side of the hill,' Scully had told him with awe yesterday. 'Where the cows have laid and flattened the long grass. Made a warm patch. We see'd them there Sat'day last.' It had brought back to Albert the uncertain memory of his own amazement when inside a book a teacher lent him, there was a strong, black body hair.

He vomited neatly into the weeds by the back fence. Tidy because it was an old habit. And he thought of himself as the little boy, stuffing a hanky into his mouth, learning to retch, while his old grey trainer looked on and laughed saying, 'You'll learn, you'll learn boy.'

Through the open door Albert could see Adelaine moving round, fixing things up before leaving and his mother's flat and oval face. Soon they'd all be going to his bed, where he was meant to be, to say goodbye. He went to the side verandah and walked back. The corner lattice was bent and falling.

Coming home had filled him with a sharp, nervous feeling. It was as if he had longed for the homecoming too hard. Reality was full of disappointments — his shuffling, sad mother, his own unease with the children he'd looked forward to meeting so much.

Albert lay on his back in bed, flexing his shoulder ligaments in a cautious test of strength. To mend properly his shoulders should be flat for another week at least but he didn't have enough time. He'd catch Thursday's train away. Already he'd decided, to be at Randwick for Saturday's races. Once there he would be able to pick up a few rides.

Everyone came to say goodnight. His mother held a sack full of his old riding ribbons. She said she was going to cut them into animal shapes for the kiddies to play with or for finger puppets. Her voice was accusing and petulant. 'The moths are only getting fat on them here.'

Behind her the sky, the trees, were colouring darkly. Albert's mother described the shapes of the animals: fish, birds, dogs, with empty fingers. The sack on the ground, the early, high moon, repeated the curve of her hands.

Adelaine's child stood watching. Albert saw the light streaming under her skin and thought of how she would play with the toys, his coloured felt ribbons cut and sewn, the fractured names of old shows in yellow writing.

'She's a happy old bugger, our Gramma,' Adelaine's daughter trembled with laughter that turned to tears as Adelaine walloped her for her rudeness. Albert saw his niece, brimming with tears and hurt, and knew that nothing was fair.

Ride A Cock Horse

The shoppers cramming through the heavy glass doors, reminded Albert of retreating bees. The bees that panicked ahead of the old hand mower Christopher Wetherstone Clark used to push round his front yard every second week, because his mother was a fussy bugger when it came to grass. Now the kikuyu and paspalum had covered her grave and the grass edged the cement with thin, mysterious patterns. Albert saw the long grass the day he searched out the location of his own parents' headstones.

The small hill with the spotty gum marking the spot had disappeared. The caretaker explained that lots of the ground had been bulldozed to make it suitable for future use. Because of all the rain the grass had gone mad, the caretaker said, reefing away at the stringy grass to reveal the old gravestone. Albert bent to read the chipped inscription of Christopher Wetherstone Clark's mother. The lead letter mouldings, much admired at the time, hadn't weathered well. Rabbit holes and subsidence made everything feel insecure. The cemetery caretaker prattled about deteriorating conditions. Albert was surprised to see her name had been Dorothy. He'd forgotton or never known. The epitaph was as vague as the past.

Sometimes, Monty would egg Albert into having a go with the mower. In summer. In Albert's memory it was always hot. The bees would gather desperately on the uncut dandelions. Inevitably some were caught in the blades. Dead or wingless but still able to sting, they lay hidden in the cut flower heads. Christopher Wetherstone Clark yelled when he trod on two at once. He blew up like a bloater toad, first his ankles, then all the way up to his face.

'You would've been dead, you silly bastard,' Albert said to the boy he'd been inventing conversations with all afternoon, if it'd been a sting anywhere nearer your neck. The doctor said . . .'

Albert half laughed from where he leaned away from the crowded street into a wall hot from the sun. For the life of him he couldn't imagine Christopher Wetherstone Clark in any other way. He was the boy just sliding into the twenty-four inch panoramic photograph a travelling photographer had taken. The photograph ended up with Albert. It was still rolled tightly inside the metal cylinder, embossed in copperplate with the photographer's four initials. When Christopher Wetherstone Clark contacted him a few weeks ago to suggest this Christmas reunion, Albert took the photograph out for a look. Christopher Wetherstone Clark was standing in the far left corner laughing at all the Ertles more formally arranged in front of the house. Because the photograph had been rolled, the skinny boy in the corner kept disappearing in the curve of thick paper. Albert thought of Christopher Wetherstone Clark like that: an elusive figure in old fashioned clothes of grey and white. Unintentionally, Albert let the picture lodge in his mind, hiding all the expressions, haircuts, clothes, laughs that he must have known once. At the same time, he was prepared to be surprised. His own family changed abruptly. When he last saw Matilda by mistake through the open louvres of a bathroom, she was naked and sagging — not a girl any more, or a new wife but into middle age with her body feeling it.

Someone had said Christopher Wetherstone Clark had lost a leg from the knee down in North Africa. Albert could easily imagine any number of flaps and wobbles that mark an injured jockey, their narrow hips busted so that in old age they'd wriggle rather than walk. But he couldn't imagine Christopher Wetherstone Clark, who had such long legs, walking with a limp, a hop, a crutch.

Last night the long black and white photograph unfurled across a dream. In the corner stood Christopher Wetherstone Clark, identical, the grin, but like a roosting bird he stood with his lower left leg missing.

Albert felt anxious for this old friend he didn't know and wouldn't recognise. Again he started to scan each face that passed, looking for fair hair. But it could have gone grey or gone altogether.

The people were knocking past Albert and the flower seller on the corner cursed as he lost a bucket of marigolds to the pavement. Bits of yellow flower were carried along by fast shoes. It was increasingly confusing to know where to look or stand. In the hot evening the bitter yellow smell of crushed petals weighed Albert down. It was stupid to be meeting. Too many years had gone since the last real farewell. Albert thought of cut dandelions and the furry bees they'd collected to use in bee races.

Outside the department store was a thin, red Father Christmas on stilts. Across the road was a low stone wall. A woman sat resting her feet as she galloped her baby on her knee to make it laugh. Albert thought he could catch the sound of her high voice singing:

Ride a cock horse to Banbury Cross
To buy little Albert a galloping horse.
It trots behind and it ambles before,
And Albert shall ride, till he can ride
No more, no more, no more, no more.

It was like his mother's voice or one of his sisters' and circled his head, monotonous as a wind-up toy.

'Ho ho ho,' the Father Christmas tried to bellow every minute or so. But it was a squeezed, sad voice and the pillow was slipping from under the red suit. Was it Christopher Wetherstone Clark? Albert thought he recognised him suddenly beneath the rouge and limp cottonwool beard. The voice wasn't familiar. Maybe it was a bit the same? Albert tried to convince himself, feeling nothing was certain.

'Ho ho ho,' wheezed Christopher Wetherstone Clark again. Albert wondered then if a one legged man could work the stilts with such agility. And also, what an old Buttery worker from way back was doing being a Father Christmas on stilts at the end of a 100 degree day.

The stilts were moving carefully among the shoppers who barely seemed to notice. Not even the children seemed interested in his gloomy pronouncements of Christmas cheer. Unsure of how to attract his attention, Albert climbed onto the ledge of the store window. The extra height gave him a few feet over the people below. Behind him a tea party of china dolls, surrounded by marching tin men, spun in a revolving light display. And then the long, sad Father Christmas, who was Christopher Wetherstone Clark, winked.

The slow wink lifted Albert's spirits. 'You sly dog,' he yelled. 'You didn't say you'd be in disguise.'

'Work. Not long to go. Come round to the back lane.'

Before the post office bells began to ring, Christopher Wetherstone Clark was moving away from the congested shop front. Another Father Christmas appeared, more genuinely corpulent with a broken veined nose and chin. Albert almost wished for a pair of stilts himself. It would have been an easier way to meet. To walk upright and high, above the milling shoppers. Still perched on the window ledge, Albert watched as the two Father Christmases passed each other. Albert jumped down, hurt his knees, and had to hurry to catch the stilts. The sun caught in the hair of people going the other way and framed Christopher Wetherstone Clark with fuzzy edges.

By the time Albert reached the back of the shop, Christopher Wetherstone Clark was dismantling his costume and unstrapping the stilts. Albert slowed down in anticipation of the missing leg. The long pieces of timber fell against the fence and Albert thought the man in the red suit was like a praying mantis as he landed on one leg and hopped to regain balance. But there were no missing bits. Albert was astonished. He'd been so prepared for the loose falling trouser leg.

'Bugger me dead,' said Albert. 'Well stone the crows. I thought you were meant to be minus a leg.'

Christopher Wetherstone Clark looked down at the rumoured missing limb and laughed.

Albert looked down too. 'Thought you only had the five toes left!'

'No, it wasn't a leg,' he pulled off the crimson cap, at the same time reaching forward to shake hands. Albert saw then that it was an ear that was lost.

'Always were a big juggy.'

'Yep, I reckon they were!'

Together, they laughed awkwardly. Their hands exchanged sweat. Albert thought of the mingling of their blood years ago, inspired by Rin Tin Tin, the Dog Actor and David Lee, Child Wonder in *The Frozen River*. Some long name like that. For a whole week Beetle was forced into playing the heroic part, while Albert and Christopher Wetherstone Clark took turns at being David Lee, hero of dangerous and frozen rivers. Beetle nearly drowned when they threw him in the creek for the scene demanding a rescue in an iced over river. Albert could recall leaping into the stagnant creek water, warm and hyacinth choked, to pull up Beetle who'd sunken tail first through the purple lilies.

'A pig dog who can't swim,' Christopher Wetherstone Clark had laughed from his dry position in the willow tree.

'Warm,' said Christopher Wetherstone Clark.

'Bit warm for all that isn't it?' Albert waved a hand at the red velvet suit.

'It is, but bloody good money to walk on stilts this time of year. Better than Easter when they expect me to dress like a rabbit.' Christopher Wetherstone Clark pulled out the pillow so the suit fell baggy around his body. His face was thick and painted. Albert could see little under the facial paint that resembled the old photo or any of his other fragile memories.

When Christopher Wetherstone Clark whisked an oily rag across his face, everything became blearier still. Unrecognisable.

At first they retold familiar stories, laughing a bit too much and sweating more. Albert was the first to feel uncomfortable. Albert's unease was increased by not being able to call Christopher Wetherstone Clark by any name. Christopher Wetherstone Clark was a boy's name and absurd for the strained and drooping figure next to him.

Christopher Wetherstone Clark's memories of memories dawdled inside Albert's head. He tried to listen carefully but it was noisy in the corner pub and he couldn't remember. Albert changed the subject by asking if Christopher Wetherstone Clark had seen the new Queen of England. It was almost a year since her visit and a new portrait hung to the left of the Tolley's Brandy clock.

'Yes,' Christopher Wetherstone Clark lifted his glass to the face in the frame. 'Our Queen. She passed by. I saw the white glove, shook a stilt. I was a February clown.'

'I rode in the Queen Elizabeth Stakes,' Albert said. 'On one of the favourites too but did no bloody good. Just as well,' he twiddled his small feet on the stool. 'Bloody Podmore rode the winner. An outsider. He had to meet her, poor bugger. Should of seen him. Anyone would've thought he'd killed not ridden a long shot to the front.' Albert remembered standing in a corner of the saddling enclosure with the other jockeys to watch the presentation. The heels of the Queen's shoes sank a bit into the steaming turf. Albert thought she was too blue and white looking. Her hair was bonnetted like the soft pink pig from the bacon advertisement.

'Still riding winners are you?' asked Christopher Wetherstone Clark.

'Haven't been going too badly,' lied Albert. More frequently now he was feeling tired and irritable. The la de dah Sydney crowds were getting him down. He hated the sharp peering faces and the women in silly hats exclaiming over the shining horses and dwarfed men.

By the time they left the pub, Christopher Wetherstone Clark was more cheerful, ho humming with enthusiasm. The street was warm still. Far away fireworks exploded and were whipped up by the sky and the spikey stars. The colours were too clear, bursting open like frozen explosions; the night overful with memory and things forgotten. The strain of all the missing years, impossible to dispel, flattened between them. It stayed there as they walked. Albert following, bandy and fast stepped, then Albert ahead briefly, Christopher Wetherstone Clark behind. In the silence that wound between them, Albert's knee creaked and popped — small penny bunger noises that Christopher Wetherstone Clark mistook for airborn beetles.

When they reached a cross street, Christopher Wetherstone Clark was leading. He stopped outside the corner terrace lit up with fairy lights and inside, beyond the narrow corridor, a large Christmas tree. They walked in with a feeling of mutual guilt, the same as years ago when they watched the bulls groaning over cows, roosters squashing hens or old Winkle McTaggart on top of his wife in the middle of the day, seen through the timber slats of a verandah blind.

The room was arranged as if for a family Christmas. Six

women were dressed like little girls or fairies but clustered in a contrived group about the Christmas tree. Real pine needles were dying on the floor. Through the other smells of eau de cologne, food and the danker odour of old, spent sweat, Albert could smell the tree.

They sat down uneasily at a table spread with a crimson cloth. Fat candles burned. The yellow wax had formed strange, contorted shapes next to the torn turkey carcass. Two other men, heavy in comparison to Albert and Christopher Wetherstone Clark, sat facing each other across the turkey. Some earlier customer, or maybe the man with the grease down his chin, had ripped away the parson's nose to suck and chew. The fragile bones lay in a wet patch on the cloth. The turkey was a shell — the hanging flesh a purple and grey colour.

Christopher Wetherstone Clark made his move quickly. For the toilet he said, but the girl he'd been talking to went with him. The women began to ask Albert for Boxing Day Cup tips. Albert mentioned his ride in the fifth — Miriam's Dream. Perhaps one of the girl's names was Miriam because there was some laughter. Albert looked into the tree. It seemed respectable. Except for the parcels under the tree that were too flimsy looking with dents in their sides, Albert could almost imagine a family Christmas.

One of the fat men took a girl and disappeared. The other man who'd written down Albert's tips on a tatty form guide swivelled in order to stare belligerently at the women left.

'Who doesn't want a jockey tonight then,' he said, crunching off the top of a drumstick to suck at the red marrow inside. Albert's skin pimpled over like the turkey skin hanging off the edges of the carving plate. It was best to stare up into the tree, not to think of all the other rooms, though never before at Christmas. In the higher branches were witchballs, fairy crowns, a small gold trumpet. There were chocolate coins in gold foil and fragile bells that looked as though they could break if there were any windows or wind. But it was a shut away house. Conversation died. There was just one window but its glass was clouded so that it neither reflected the scene within or was transparent to the street and houses outside. It was impossible to see out of and in the end the only place to look was beneath the lower branches. A woman picked up a wooden recorder and started to play shrill carols. Albert watched her until halfway through *Christmas tree, o Christmas tree*, she stopped abruptly to stare back. Albert felt the hostility, even as the pink, pointing tongue tickled provocatively the tip of the recorder. She stood up, so hot, tired, bored, Albert knew, but he followed her, inside his trousers, the unwrinkling already beginning. Ahead of them lumbered the fat man with a brown haired woman. Albert glanced back at the tree. The frosted glass icicles looked ready to expire. And from where it was impaled at the top of the tree, the pinched and naked fairy seemed to falter or droop.

A striped Christmas stocking at the end of the bed shocked Albert as well as the nursery rhyme, *Ride a Cock Horse*, that galloped out of control in his head. Afterwards, he felt compelled into contributing something extra into the sock. He dug round in his pockets for coins, only finding the jelly jubes he'd bought earlier to give to Sid and Majella's daughter. He dropped them in.

'Got the time?' she reefed the fairy suit over her head.

'One o'clock,' Albert replied, thinking.

Bell horses, bell horses, what time of day? One o'clock, one o'clock, time to away.

It was how running races had started when he was a little blighter at Sports Days. Instead of trophies, winners were given bells and ribbons.

Albert almost collided with the gigantic stomach of a man, hurrying like himself, away from the bedrooms. Albert looked down the hall, hoping to sight Christopher Wetherstone Clark but there was no sign. The man in front farted and kicked up one leg as though to boot the smell away. Which made the man windy all over again only this time he cow kicked the air with his other leg. Too much turkey seasoning, thought Albert, as his own bowels contracted. He turned around to find the toilet.

Christopher Wetherstone Clark was there, staring in the small mirror.

'Time for bed,' Albert watched his widdle stream like rain in the gutter.

Christopher Wetherstone Clark just nodded. Had he always been so silent? They looked at each other in the mirror, not knowing what to say, their flaccid faces full of odd shadows. Albert sensed all remnants of a friendship slipping into the humid, soapy smell of the room. He felt the sadness of time. Where Christopher Wetherstone Clark's ear should have been, was a twisted dark entrance. In the perfumed light Albert imagined its dark tunnels. On the outside all that was left was a thin reef of hair.

They went back into the corridor, stomping along and clearing their throats to save talking. A new shift of fairy girls had arrived. A new group of men too and a plump, untouched turkey. One man still pulled at the last shreds of meat on the old carcass. A woman sat on his knee waving her wand. The man yelled he'd found the wishbone. Unfairly, he hooked his little finger around the knob at the base of the bone. With a crack, it snapped in his favour.

Albert and Christopher Wetherstone Clark kept walking. A bowl of fruit salad placed right at the end of the table looked dirty with slowly discolouring circles of banana. Christopher Wetherstone Clark drifted into the entrance hall. Albert was close behind. He looked back to where the Christmas tree was lean and sad looking, bending into the corner. Wall paper peeling from the top down had nearly reached the fairy on top.

Outside, they separated. The footpath had lost no heat. It came through their shoes so their socks would smell when taken off. Under a signpost, they shook hands quickly, not holding each other's fingers long enough to feel the dull, satiated pulse of thumb.

The pink house lights gave Albert's face a weepy, lost look. He felt old and unsatisfied. *Ride a Cock Horse*. Nursery rhymes were for children, not aching jockeys. But it wouldn't leave his head, persisting and gloomy. *And Albert shall ride, till he can ride no more, no more, no more.*

Dwarfed

I want my flat chest back. Lying in the bath they wobble if I move even a bit. They are kind of funny I suppose but I don't want them. The Cheesemite says they're like beer bottle tops. I think they do look like that if they're wet, or if I blow on them. Like snapdragons shutting up when you put your fingers inside, or a hairy caterpillar shrinking on the top of a burning log. I don't wear a bra. I never want to. The Cheesemite says I will have to though if I want to keep on riding. He says they'll be at my belly button in no time otherwise.

The Cheesemite is one of this town's oldest residents and heroes. When I think about it he is in fact the only hero. He has met the queen. In the fifties, when he was a top jockey. The queen shook his hand with a white glove and said How do you dooo, like Eliza Doolittle in this book we did at school. It was on television. I only watched as far as Eliza being able to speak like royalty before Mum threw a fit and switched channels. She said what garbage and settled back to watch some serial that always makes her sad. That's my mother for you. She's watching the television now and thankgoodness for that. I can have my bath in peace! It is unbelievable how she goes on about me washing the horse brushes in the bath. She's a real fusspot about this kind of thing and says I will catch something. What a laugh. If anyone's doing something stupid then it's her. Where Dad piddles over the veranda at night, all the elephant leaves grow speckled. And my mother tries to get the spots off. On her knees, scrubbing away at them with the kitchen wipers that are too old to use on the dishes. I think she must think they're some removable species of leaf blight. She'd never believe the truth so I've never told her. I don't think even Dad would know I've seen him. I can tell he really enjoys doing it: in spurts and staring beyond the yellow arc. Sometimes he tries to hit down the big spider webs. So far as I know, he hasn't been successful yet.

I wouldn't like to be a spider or an ant in our garden. My mother goes round killing ants with Ant Rid, the brown ones on the cement and in cracks. I like ants — the little brown ones. Once, sitting on the verandah where the sun comes in, I found an ant grave where all the dead ones are carried to. They were piled up in a curved hollow near the wall. I scooped them out with my finger. They were lighter than anything I've ever felt. They blow or crumble away in the end. Hopefully they died of natural causes rather than Piperonyl Butoxide.

I can feel sad for dead ants, or dead mice for that matter. At the Cheesemite's place, mice get in the molasses if I leave the lid off over night. Then I have to pick them out but it's a most terrible feeling. In the mornings the molasses is so cold and thick. I can tell if there's one in there because of a lump in the shiny black surface. Usually they are tail down. I know then they've died struggling to get out, their pointed noses only just below the molasses. By the time I get to them, they are hard balls with stiff little arms each side, but I still can't remember to put that lid on. The Cheesemite says I will forget my head one of these days.

The Cheesemite is not really called that. I only call him that in my mind. I call him nothing much when I go there. His real name is Mr Ertle. He looks like Rumple-stiltskin I think. I call him the Cheesemite because ever since he stopped being a jockey he eats heaps and heaps of cheese. He says it's because he wasn't allowed to before. It would've made him fat. He's got fat now. Not exactly fat all over. It's as if only his middle has realised it's not still starving. Jockeys have to starve. One chop is all he could eat every night. One round lamb chop with peas and no mashed potato or gravy. That's why he eats so much cheese. He can eat as many as two giant blocks of Kraft Processed in a week and a half. I like cheese in thin pieces. He slices it off his slab for me with his pocket knife. Fatty and Skinny is what he calls us.

Fatty and Skinny went to the zoo
Fatty got lost in the elephant's poo.

He laughs when I say that. My Dad says he's an okay fellow. My mother says he's a dirty old man and ought to be put down. He is the best bloke I have ever known.

After me and the Cheesemite finish exercising the horses on weekends we go up to the house and maybe make tomato jam if it's the tomato season. I like to pick tomatoes, I like the smell of their leaves. They have soft skins and sweet insides. Tomato jam is the Cheesemite's specialty. At first it looks terrible. Mashing it is the worst part. He rolls up both sleeves and I can see how many muscles are still in his arms. Then he adds plenty of salt, pepper and sugar. The windows all steam up and we have tea out of white china mugs that are stained brown inside. The Cheesemite says you get a better cup of tea by not scrubbing this out. I would say he's right. In winter the fat old pot belly stove will be muttering away in the corner and slowly our toes start warming up inside our boots. They freeze if the leather of riding boots gets soaked through in the wet grass. You really know it then if a horse stomps on a foot.

The Cheesemite is training me for jumping. It's the Sports Day tomorrow and most of all I want to beat Tanya Musgrove. She's my enemy at school. She says I have big ears and can make me go bright red just by shrieking at me, 'You're going red, you're going red.' She's not a very good rider and the Cheesemite says I will be jake no worries at all.

That's what else my breasts look like: tomato seeds, the ones stuck round the edges of the saucepan when the jam is almost cool and ready to eat. Not when they're like this, all smooth and pink-brown, but when they scrunch up. I can make them do this by pinching the top of them. The little bumps pop up quickly. They won't go like it tonight.

I should get out of this bath but as the television is still going I'm safe for the moment. I like to have a bath. I never can feel my fingers or feet crinkling but they always do. When I was small I once stayed in a tree all afternoon, waiting to see the streetlights blinker on. I sat there three whole hours and missed the exact moment. It is the same with fingers in the bathwater: one moment they seem quite ordinary, the next time I look it has happened.

Oh-oh, I think I hear my mother coming. She wears old pink slippers with bent rabbit ears. The sort only little kids should wear. She shuffles along in them over the floorboards. I always leave it too late to let the water out and grab for a towel. She has noticed my growing chest and has got into the habit of commenting. She calls them little lemons. And she points out my growing forest under each arm. Three wispy hairs.

It's a pity to be forcefully evicted from a bath. I find it hard to believe the dictator in her light blue bomber suit dressing gown used to sing the *Rub a Dub Dub, Three Men in a Tub*, song to me. But there are photos and I know the rhyme. *The butcher, the baker, the candlestick maker* . . .

She's plodding along the hall tonight which probably means there'll be no nonsense. She'll come in, pull the plug and tell me not to use up all the hot water.

I've had a reprieve. Dad is calling for tea and toast. Good on you Dad. Yes, it's for sure. I can hear the lid being rattled off the teapot and the jar of honey unsticking from the top shelf. I don't like honey by the time it's three quarters gone and afloat with crust crumbs and fat lumps of butter. It's enough to make a person sick.

Come to think of it, I eat most things and most of all

at the Cheesemite's. Riding the horses makes me starving. His garden is dark with fruit trees and mulberries. There are grapes, mandarin trees, cumquats — only good for jam, as well as the biggest locquat tree in town.

The round locquat seed fits perfectly in a rolled up tongue. Good ammunition. It used to be fun to crouch in the dog house and try and hit the Cheesemite's boots as he went past. It's nice inside there: smells of the dark and of old bones and the sacks on the floor aren't prickly because so many dogs over the years have flattened them out. All you can hear inside is the sound of the Cheesemite's budgies talking away to each other. The aviary is just the other side of the kennel. It's not a wooden kennel with a roof like you see in books, but big pieces of corrugated iron jammed together. Like the Cheesemite's house it's a little bit crooked. He says the fleas don't get me because I'm so skinny.

I haven't thought much about being skinny but I suppose I am, although my legs are getting fatter. All the girls at school are starting to pinch at your shoulders to see if there's a bra underneath. Angela Pearce was wearing one in Primary!

I hope mine never reach the size of my mother's. When she's wearing a bra they are really huge. She wears a cannon ball brand of bra. Even though her breasts are as saggy as old cabbage leaves, they poke out once she manouvres them into place. Projectile breasts. Her bras are shiny and in photos show through her shirt. Even when the bra is lying empty on the bed it has two big points all by itself. When she takes off her bra after the Saturday morning shop, there are red stripes where the straps have cut into her skin. That's how heavy her breasts are.

If the Cheesemite says I should wear a bra then I suppose I must. I'm the only person he allows to ride his horses and I don't want to go all floppy. There is something else too. I can feel them growing now as I ride, especially trotting. Or going over a bump on my bike. I used to have a chest. Now I'm getting breasts. Tanya Musgrove stuffs her bra with tissues to fill out her riding coat. I've seen her doing it with toilet paper.

I'd better win the jumping tomorrow or the Cheesemite and me will both be disappointed. I've been riding Punch every morning before school for four weeks now as well as every afternoon. He's going beautifully. I arrive on my bicycle when the mist is blue it's so early. Sometimes if I'm late I have to jump out of bed, put jeans over my pyjamas and peddle like mad. And when he sees me hurtling past the yards he calls me his little Red Riding Hood on account of my pyjamas and beanie being bright wool red.

Punch will be saddled up ready with an old rug thrown over him so he doesn't catch cold. After a bit of flat work we might put up a few jumps. We do it properly with real white wings and painted poles that I helped to do last year. Then he'll ring his brass bell that's green inside and I will salute him just as if he's a real jumping judge, which he often is.

'On your merry way,' the Cheesemite will say, and if I fall off, he'll say, 'What did you hop off for.' It's hard to laugh when you're winded, but I had to laugh when he said that.

His squashed up hat is smeared with molasses streaks. He is never without this hat, or his baggy mole-skins. If I do something stupid he'll waggle those salt and pepper eyebrows one at a time in my direction. His eyes leak like ripe mulberries in the morning. I look at them watering and red and find it hard to see him as someone who was once my age. He can always tell the time by the sun. Never wrong.

Come to think of it, it's time I got out of this bath. The skin round my toenails is wrinkled and white. I've also run all the hot water out. Now I'll really be in trouble. There's nothing like a good long bath but once this luke-warm stage is reached, I've had enough.

66

It's the same temperature as the river in summer. Often me and the Cheesemite go out in the dinghy to swim any racehorse he might have in training. He likes to tell me the names and bloodlines of good horses he rode. The names roll from him in time with the putt-putting engine. I dangle my fingers in the warm ripples from the boat. The Cheesemite makes me laugh. Sometimes I reckon the horse we're swimming looks to be laughing too. I know really that all horses lift their top lip when swimming but sometimes it can seem like they're grinning away.

Valiant Prince, Swift River, Silver Pete, Our Paddy, The Dancer . . . the old names make the Cheesemite happy. *Sweet Hopes, Star Maid, Bobby Luck.* The wrinkles in his face stretch and laugh and spread widely like the early morning river all around us.

II

I can't help crying. My mother says I'm overwrought and over tired which shows how much she knows about her only daughter. I don't know why my mother has to be like that — such a nagger, always picking me to pieces. As if she knows everything. Tonight she said I'd have to give up this horse nonsense if this is what it does to me.

Dad is worse in a way. He tries hard but ends up embarrasing everyone. Because he insists on bringing lunch to shows rather than buying hot chips like everyone else I have to eat thick vegemite sandwiches. There's always so much vegemite the top of my mouth stings. He cheers me along and people stare. I know everyone is laughing. The Cheesemite calls my parents The Two Ravers. This is all they do, rave and rave. I'm thankful not to have inherited their capacity to go on boiling their cabbages about something, anything, everything.

Tears falling in the water are sad and silent. I lean forward and they plop in dismal circles. If I sit really still and don't breathe, the bath water becomes quiet. Except tonight I can't stop crying. In the silver of the bath tap I bloat and elongate like something monstrous. It's impossible to stop the hiccoughs and sadness. The kind of crying that hurts my chest. There is runny nose all over the place, snot on my left breast. When I reach this stage it seems my shoulders and face can keep on crying without me thinking. Just on and on.

Honey my dog is the only one who cares. She has pushed open the door with her nose to come and say hello. She likes to drink hot water out of my cupped hands. Her tongue is warm, red and long. The Cheesemite says she is one big mutt. I wonder if I can still call him that. It sounds babyish, sweet and sick.

I could die in my bath water and no one would discover me until the morning. The water would get cold, then my body and I'd blow up like a toad. It's a deep, green bath tub — coffin shaped to drown in.

The soap has fallen in and gets slimy. I might as well leave it there. Punch was a champion today, a real champ. He behaved like a gentleman but tried as hard as he could. Lots of people commented to me about how well he was looking. Today was the last show for the year — a good Sports Day really. Although it's not much of a town and the school toilets are wooden seated, this town's show is the best around. I hate those toilet seats. The piddle has been sinking into them for over half a century.

My mother says crying is only part of growing up and becoming a woman. What bullshit. I'm not growing up and as if that is anything to do with anything anyway. She wouldn't know. The moment I saw her tonight she asked about the jockey pisspot. And she wonders why I don't feel like pea and ham soup.

The Cheesemite has dealt me a rough hand. After the show was winding up I went looking for him. I felt so good. We were going to watch some of the night time events like we always do. Because he's so small he can sit on the round flat posts either side of the open air stand like I can. But he wasn't at the bar and someone said he'd gone home.

· I thought maybe he'd be cooking some pancakes. He makes the best pancakes this world has ever seen. I walked Punch from the showground. There were stars and a smell of nightsmoke. Burning leaves or something bitter.

When I arrived the car was there and the kitchen light on. I gave Punch a giant feed for being such a winner. On my way to the house I picked some strawberries. They can be seen in the dark if you push the leaves back to look for the green white undersides.

But the Cheesemite wasn't there. The kitchen door was open and there was a heap of bugs and moths. Wrong way up on the table was his hat. Never before have I seen it off his head. I picked it up to smell inside. A peculiar mouse smell, grease and hair. I put it on my head to surprise him. As he wasn't in the back room I crept right to the door of the bedroom. First time ever in that corner of the house but I'd run out of places to look.

It was ridiculous. I knew what they were doing immediately. The Cheesemite and me have laughed enough times when Flapper comes on heat and the dogs come from everywhere, trying so hard to get on top of her before the Cheesemite's boot sends them yelping.

This was too much. A woman. She was on top of HIM! The tiny little Cheesemite. He was being squashed by this great wobble jelly bum. I squeaked. My head itching with sweat and between my legs and under my arms. But it didn't matter. She was making enough noise to deafen an army. She sat upright then, right on top of the Cheesemite who was squirming away underneath, and started bouncing up and down, up and down, up and down. She still had a bra on.

Black and lacey it was and she stopped for a second to take it off. Her breasts. They made me choke on my strawberry. Wopping. Giants in the world of breasts. Then something went wrong. I could tell something went wrong. She got off, put her head down and began licking away at him. Honestly she did.

Which is when I ran. He looked so stupid. Like a frog that's had its legs run over. Albert Thomas Ertle. A. T. Ertle. A turtle! Upside down and stuck.

I can't get over that woman's boobs, breasts. Mine are so piddly in comparison. Dwarfed. They have gone all pointy by themselves. I don't know what I'll do when I see him. I think when my mother comes to turf me out of this bath I'll ask her about bras. You can get them at Randalls I'm pretty sure.

The tap dripping on my feet beats time with my pulse. Seventy two pumps in sixty seconds. If I put my big toe over the tap the water builds up until it squirts in every direction. Then dribbles. Then drips again. In time with tears.

When I was in kindergarten I used to look straight at a light and then screw my eyes up as hard as I could. Then there would be explosions of colours and revolving circles, from greens and yellows into deeper purple. That is what I'm doing now. The light is very strong but it still works — colours in my mind, small yellow suns.

Rosemarion

Walking past the fruit store I can smell the strawberries turning dark and soft and violent. The bottoms of furry peaches flatten and stick to the hot cardboard hollows. Elbeth Merriwhether has put out a new sign in her trembling writing, to reduce strawberry punnets by ten cents. They're beyond being good for jam even, but their smell is thick and enticing long after I've walked by.

That's the way smells work in summer. I go past a shop but it's not until the next shop is reached that the odours of the previous one come to me. The Rosemarion Pie Shop is a good example. The dry, dusty air catches the tastes of the yellow flavouring that makes the custard slices and lemon tarts look so bright. There's a smell of warm butter and cinnamon. In the display window the dough of fat cream buns attracts the flies and a mound of flaking cream horns makes it hard to choose. FANCY BREAD, says the chipped blue sign overhead but it's not the burnt tank loaves making people linger at the window.

From the nose and thumbprints smudging the glass I see I'm not the first person to back track here this morning. The MacDermont sisters join me, their cotton print dresses bulging round big bottoms as they lean so close to the glass — pointing and conferring before pushing through the plastic streamer door. Nothing stops people in the street the way the smells of the cake shop can.

A bag of currant rock cakes is very filling but nowhere near as good as two neenish tarts, a bargain at three cents less. Finally I decide on the neenish tarts, one caramel nut slice and two cream horns. They're wrapped separately, then swung altogether in a white paper bag.

The cakes are a perfect weight in my hand. I almost collide with Teddie Arthurs coming into the shop with his Mum. A scraggly pair. Teddie looks like his mother with short cropped hair the colour of browned-off grass. I grin at him but he doesn't do anything back. He has queer eyes, so big and black in that white face of his. The headlice has sucked too much blood from his brain I reckon. I wait till I'm out of the door before shaking my head. Nits can hop fifteen feet or more to settle behind your ears and breed. His moony face peers through the coloured door-streamers and makes me hitch at my blouse. It's a new shirt with embroidered flowers and an elastic top that will slide down over my shoulders.

My bike's at the end of the street.

I cross over to the other side so I'll be walking in the shade. I smell the butcher's shop coming up and hold my breath. It has the worst smell and stronger as the day warms up.

'Going to be a scorcher,' says a man I don't know. I nod yes. The flowering jacarandas are a deeper blue and swelling against the sky. Under the man's arm is a lump of meat wrapped in white paper — already it's leaking. His other hand pockets his change. I can see the blood from the butcher's hands still on the notes. Probably if I looked really close I'd see small particles of meat on the money. But he's past me now and ahead the meat carrier is hulking a pig carcass from the back of the refrigerated van. He wears a white apron and a cap with old, red marks like a brand at the front. The pig's legs swing out and almost clunk me one, so the strong meat smell is close and heavy and cold to me. Inside the van three other bodies hang blue, pink and white, on steel hooks. Through the thick glass window of the Butcher's, the meat chopper rises and drops in sharp rhythms through a rump of beef. The jolly face of an apprentice is blurred and smiling. He needs a bullet if he thinks that's fun.

72

Red, white blue, the boys love you.
They took you to the Butcher's Shop,
And undressed you.

Here is a candle to light you to bed.
And here comes The Chopper to chop off your head.
Chip Chop. Chip chop. Chip chop.

Old nursery rhymes take on new meanings as you grow up. When the butcher's son tried to kiss me I made him bleed: bit his tongue at the school dance and tasted his ginger blood. He's become the Glint-Chinker of my new nightmares. *Chip chop, chip chop,* chasing me for hours through the night with a silver knife, his red hair on end he runs so fast. Freckles the colour of blood.

'I eat raw steak,' he boasted. 'I chew it like gum until it goes white.'

The metal band strapping his teeth was horrible and the way he said he'll be getting me back, no problems, for biting like a cat.

It's later than I thought because the big families slow to begin Saturday morning, straggle down the street. I hurry off, not looking at the armless man who sits on a camp stool outside the empty lot selling pens. His shoulders end in soft pink flaps that snout from his shirt. I can't remember a time when he wasn't there.

'Help the handicapped please,' he spits and flaps his shoulders like a baby chicken.

I catch smells of new saddles and then the burnt hair of old ladies under the dome shaped setters of the hairdresser's. My bike's just beyond Jane's Hair Salon. It looks maimed where it has fallen over and the handlebars have skewed a little bit to the right. The seat's hot and burns through my skirt. Riding by the pub I get the feeling of being looked at by old men with blue noses. I tug at my shirt. My shoulders are smooth and brown like knobs of well polished wood and from somewhere high up comes a loud man whistle. Without moving my head I try to spot him but he's invisible and it's good to turn the corner away from town and towards the river. Now it's alright to let my shirt slip. It tickles where the elastic creeps down to let the air in.

Under the bike wheels the long bells of jacaranda flowers are squashing and bruising. Below every large tree lies a circle of fallen blooms. On the melting road they heat and collapse in strange, mauve patterns.

I ride no hands so I can dip a finger into the melting insides of a cream horn. By the time I reach The Old Creamery Road all that's left is the outside pastry and I eat that too. It's salty and I let the flakes dissolve bit by bit on my tongue. This far out of town, the jacarandas have thinned and it's only tar bubbles popping now against the bike wheels. Across the ricketty wood bridge, I slow down to see the hyacinth clogging the creek. There's a drying wind but a neenish tart keeps my mouth moist. The icing is thick and colourful like the day. It's the pastel time of year. Roses, old fashioned hydrangeas, lupins and early agapanthus, purple the gardens and the jacarandas are thick this year with flower. The full heat of the summer is almost here and everything is washed and fading in preparation. Pastel and pale yellow skies begin and end each day. School goes on but it's hardly noticeable. I've seen the horses are getting grass bellies and turning yellow on their long summer spell and Mr Ertle sleeps on his verandah where it's cool. For homework I had to look up a word — stanchless. A word without colour I thought: blanched like the badly pressed jacaranda flowers I found in the back pages of the dictionary. I've forgotten ever putting them there. There's a hollow in my memory and it's filled with mould and purple flowers.

The river is around the next bend. I ride faster in expectation. Bamboo clumps and the fig that's over a century old mark my destination. It's such a disappointment to see another bike at my spot. Soon it'll be too stinking hot to come all the way out. Perhaps this is the last weekend I'll feel like making the effort. If only I'd got up earlier there'd be no one here before me.

I don't recognise the bike. It's a boy's bike, rusty and blue. There's a strand of tinsel tied to the handle bar. A festive sort of bike with its wheels sunk in sand. I make a lot of noise, trying to flush him out, ring the bell on his bike. Nobody appears. I yell and get no reply.

The river water is muddy and warm in the shallows and I hope I'm not swallowing down the water where the man with the bike has drowned. But I'm so thirsty I can't care, drinking in big gulps with my lips to the water like a horse. Then my nose, forehead and all my hair goes under too. The waterline clings around my thighs. Under my shirt I feel my belly round and tight with all the water inside. I'm water bloated and ready for the pastries. A hump of sand is a good headrest. The cream and jam has warmed up more then ever in the sun but it adds to the taste. Hot and sugary it brings out the vanilla taste. I like to separate flavours in this way.

When I've finished all but a neenish tart, I feel sick and hot, my blood boiling with sugar. A vein pulses at the blue pen message near my inside elbow, reminding me of something that had to be done. It looks important; spindly capitals and the deep violet vein below. Indecipherable though.

I lie backwards and see the sky, blue and furrowing move towards me. A high noon sky. There are black birds and blue patterns. When I flop onto my front there's a pair of feet lying in the slats of cane shadow. From this angle I see right up his shorts and there are no underpants — just two thinly haired lumps, purple or darker, the colour of eggs boiled black. And a bright dot, just like the red eye found unexpectedly in a ferti-lised chook egg at breakfast. Is it a pimple? Do boys get pimples there?

He's fast asleep and has the face of an angel. Nothing at all like Wayne the butcher's son whose chin is erratic with a new beard breaking through a hundred and one blackheads.

An ant is climbing the slender hairs under the knees. I see smooth nipples and the pulse of his heart. I'd like to run my finger up the ridge of bone behind the rim of ear, it's so delicate. The sand squeaks as I move closer and he shifts a bit. Sand falls off his shoulder to reveal a birthmark. It is lavender coloured and the shape of a butterfly wing. It's sort of pretty. Only the dried wriggle of snot in his left nostril is annoying. I inch closer, belly crawling through the cane until I'm lying so close we're exchanging sweat. I turn onto my back, see before us our bogged bikes, the vertical weaving of young bamboo and don't know how I've dared to take his hand. His skin is dry and I feel my sweat hot in the lines that map my palms. Lying backwards and horizontal I hold his hand tight, like I'm watching a film in the sky with my boyfriend right beside me. 'Lovely,' I whisper. 'Love a lee,' saying the word slowly so that it is.

I'm thumping inside. I'm thudding into the sand my heart's beating so fast. He's slightly burnt on his stomach and his belly button is a white circle in the middle. There's fluff inside. I sit up to see better and my top slips half way down but I don't care. If I arch my back I can make my breasts look bigger. I pull out his belly button lint. It smells of washing flapping in the wind. I go to sleep because it's so hot lying in the sun.

Not all that much later when I wake up his shorts are on the ground. He's wearing green dicksticker speedos. His tassle pokes out of them into the whispering air. He's sleeping again. I think he is. My nipples are sore from the sun. I pull my top right up over the shoulders and try to disengage my hand. It seems his fingers are tightening. Is he asleep? His hairline is damp and curling. I stroke a piece of cane and feel it hollow and deaf. It's silent inside and his hand won't let go of mine. I see very faraway, the chimneys of town. I look for something burning, a smoke cloud, a column, a rescue, a message. The flame tree at the edge of town near Mr Ertle's tricks me for a moment, bursting alight in my mind. But it's almost summer and all the winter fires have died. The chimneys are empty, the fireplaces scraped back and decorative with pine cones or dried flowers. On my arm in blue school pen there's a message I wish I could read. I'm meant to be doing something, not becoming part of an odd seduction I thought I wanted but don't want at all. Any moment now I expect his lips. If he makes me swap spit I'll become weak. When a boy spits in a puppy's mouth, it'll be loyal for life and that's why boys poke their tongues into girl's mouths. It gives them control, the right to bend heads with heavy arms looped across you in some kind of ownership, the right to poke their things into you and touch your breasts. I look again at his tassle. There's a long vein right up the middle. He doesn't look like a head bender. He looks funny. While the going seems so good, I retreat. My hand slips out of his easily. Black ants are all over the paper bag with the last neenish tart inside. I take it out and crawl back into the circle of cane to place it on his chest. The yellow and purple icing splits the cake in half. Gold and lilac are the colours of triumph — the colours of old faded jockey silks.

Awake or asleep? It's impossible to tell. Perhaps he blinks exactly in time with my eyes.

Down there between his legs, things are shrinking fast. He blinks. I'm sure he blinks and his face is almost purple. Even his chest is blushing. I see his eyes are squeezed tight. He is holding them shut. I bend towards him. 'My name is Rose Marion,' I will say, when he opens those eyes. It's not my name but it has the right sound. I run my fingers through my tangled hair, worried that maybe I'm not good enough to pass for such a pretty name. My nose is full of freckles. My legs are black and hairy because Mum still won't let me shave them. When his foot moves in the sand, I bolt for my bike. I wish I was on a horse. I peddle crazily. One of Mr Ertle's big bay thoroughbreds would be more impressive.

'Rose Marion!' I imagine the boy's voice calling, soft and blurred as the pastel sky. I peddle full pelt down the long road away from the river, and I don't look back.

Off Season

No one was around to book them into the Blue Lagoon Caravan Park. The reservations office was locked. A few onsite vans clustered near the grey circle of Hills hoists but they looked empty. Scotch thistles were growing in their aluminium stairs and the kidney shaped swimming pool was slime grown. Sidney, who had been in charge of driving all the way, thumped the wheel angrily. He'd expected more and made his brother scrabble round in the back seat to find the NRMA caravan accomodation guide.

Albert had to squint hard in the fading light to make out the small print. Next to the star hot water, electricity, no pets and laundry facilities were listed. Albert eased himself from the car to undo the gate. It was an old gate, stiff with salt rust. He laughed at the hand written sign hanging from the corner post: Colour TV, spas and electric blankets all available on a bring your own basis.

'Come on then Al. Open the bloody gate,' Sidney revved the Bedford. Sand flew, landing inside Albert's riding boots. The caravan slewed. Albert followed on foot, his eyes searching out a good spot. He could hear the sea. He dug for a lump of wax in his left ear and yelled at Sidney to stop where they'd have a view over the water. Sidney pulled up not twelve feet from the concrete amenities block, saying that he wasn't going walkabout everytime he needed a piss.

Albert opened up a family sized tin of beans for dinner and grated cheese into the saucepan to add flavour. He turned the hotplate on full and positioned three slices of bread neatly under the griller.

'Hey Sid. Want some baked beans?'

Sid grunted. Albert wondered why they were called that. Really they were boiled beans. Sidney was still hoeing into what was left of the liquorice and chewing gum from the trip. He was eating it together and swallowing down big grey lumps.

'You'll stick your stomach up,' Albert tried to warn. Sidney barely looked up. 'Just as well we're parked near the dunnies,' he said. 'After a tin of beans there's no way in the world you won't be needing a bog in the night.'

They ended up both going to the toilet at midnight because the owner of the Blue Lagoon woke them, thumping at their door. The pub had closed and he wanted five dollars before the morning in case they were planning to sneak away.

Side by side at the urinal, in profile, in the strange fluoresent blue, it seemed impossible there once had been a strong brotherly likeness. Sometimes Albert caught himself looking at Sidney, wondering could it really be his little brother grown so red and fat.

There were rotting birds all along the beach the next day. 'Must've been a storm out to sea,' Albert said.

Sidney was batting them into sand banks with a piece of driftwood. There were mutton birds as well as seagulls.

'Have to burn or bury them,' said Albert. 'Start to stink soon otherwise.'

Sidney kept swinging, pretending he was on a golfing green and making soft putting noises with his mouth. Both brothers wore felt hats and long sleeves but Albert had made one concession to the sand by leaving off his boots. Sidney was hairier than Albert but not as white. The soft sand squeaked under their pale feet. They winced crossing the high tide mark of broken shells and the sharper kelp.

Imitating the pose of a golfer, Sidney took aim and tried to putt a bird through Albert's bowed legs. It clunked the back of Albert's knee. Albert felt its beak and the wet feathers.

'Cut it out,' Albert waved a hand. 'Something's got to be done with them. They'll smell the place out.'

'Eat them,' suggested Sidney.

Albert walked on. It was a long while since the two of them had been to the beach together. Fifteen years Sidney reckoned, but it could've been longer. Albert thought it must have been at a family reunion sort of thing that one of the girls had organised. It had been his suggestion to come now. Sidney had been bored, watching country telly all day and complaining that the pub didn't open on Sundays. Albert liked the place but Sidney liked to curse it in the mornings. Their childhood town but Sidney called it hell on earth. So it was better that they stay on the coast until Majella was back and Sid could get back to Sydney. They'd have a good time. And at least the old van made the trip. Not slowly either. Sidney couldn't be told about taking corners easy.

Albert glanced at Sidney who'd hurled his wood away. They reached the end of the beach and for a while stood watching the green waves breaking close inshore. No one else was on the long beach, not even a dog. On the wet sand lay half a giant fish. Something had taken a bit out of it. Albert thought of sharks and a sudden death. Sidney was stripping down to his blue Bonds. He flopped into the rolling water while Albert took a closer look at the fish. It was fresh. He watched Sidney, noticing the white hair on his brother's chest like poisoned river weed.

'It's warm. You should come in,' Sidney floated belly up, bouyant over waves.

Albert didn't answer. He'd picked up some flat pebbles to skitter across the wash but he'd lost the knack. Finally a sea smoothed circle of white glass skidded into Sidney. Albert cheered. It had bounced on water five times.

Despite Sidney's complaints, they stayed at the Blue Lagoon. Now the summer season was ended, everywhere else had shut down. Cheap too and since Albert and Sidney were the Blue Lagoon's only visitors, the hot water never ran out. Every night Sidney would barbeque steaks while Albert made for the blue and white fish and chips shop as fast as he could go. By the time he arrived back with eighty cents worth of chips, double wrapped in white paper to keep them hot, the meat would be charring black. Sid wasn't too good with wood fires. Albert ate his steak plain, with a fried egg over the top. He cooked it so the middle was runny, the outer edges crinkling and brown. Sid preferred sour yellow mustard and tomato sauce.

There were Autumn storms and sometimes the sun was thin. The sand didn't dry until late morning but Sidney always left for the pub and snooker long before then. Sometimes Albert joined him for a game and a beer but he liked the beach. It really lived up to its name of Shelly Beach. The small tiger cowries delighted him. Many weren't damaged at all, the teeth still smooth and even. He collected the cream sea-snail shells and the slivered mother-of-pearl. Bags of grit for his budgies too. Or it was nice to sit in the sun with the papers.

But before Albert could enjoy the beach, he had to clean it up. The birds had begun to rot in the moist air. One evening soon after they'd arrived, Albert boiled a tin of soup for his thermos. It had been a soft and blurred day, the air occasionally bad with the drift of decaying birds. In the afternoon winds, the smell carried as far as the caravan park.

Albert wished he'd thought to bring something for his nose or a peg. He looked for wood first. Most of it was pale and salty, but it would burn. With care he selected a good spot for the fire; out of the wind and in sight of the sea. He built the fire his own way, using sheets of newspaper twisted and coiled in rings and building a steep igloo of twigs around them. Only then did he go to gather the birds. Reluctantly, he decided that the hessian sack doormat from the caravan would be needed.

Sand had filled the beaks and feathers of the mutton birds. It was difficult trying to keep the sack open and push the birds in with a two pronged branch. Except for the sand, everything kept falling out. The curved beaks of some sooty terns snagged in the sacking. Albert dropped the clumsy wood. There was nothing for it, he'd have to use his hands. Already the sea was shadowing with troughs. Soon the light would go.

Most of the birds had eyes that stared. Their bodies were stiff and smelly but the feathers downy under the wings. It was a large chaff sack Albert was using but even when full, there were more birds. He stacked on larger pieces of wood, adding the birds at intervals during the process. Albert didn't know why he stuffed some of them tail first through the newspaper coils. In the disappearing sun it made them look like toys — inflated birds to float with children in ponds.

Before he struck the matches, Albert scouted round for the ones he'd missed. There was a big silver gull with ants in its eyes. The feathers were fine and clean and Albert removed a couple for his hat. This bird he put into the last log he'd dragged over. He stuffed it in firmly like putty into a crack.

The matches were soggy. Pinched from a motel Albert once stayed at, they didn't look too healthy. The ends were white. Not until the sixth match did a flame strike. Once, the bottom of a boot had been enough to get a match alight.

The burning was spectacular. The flames whooshed up from the bottom just as planned. For a moment it looked like a burning tree with the eyes of birds terrified in the smoke. Then it was like Aunt Ettie's Christmas tree used to look, with all the colour and light and hidden things in the branches. In a while, when the flesh began to burn, there'd be a smell of roast lamb. Where sea salt had crusted on logs, the flames grew blue at the edges. Albert poured out his soup but the stench on his hands alarmed him. He walked down to the sea to wash it off, feeling his cold-stiffening muscles, the creak of his knee. There were hidden lights in the water. It wouldn't have been a bad night for fishing.

Still crouched by the sea, Albert turned to look at his fire. He could hear the logs popping as they collapsed inwards. The sparks were leaping high but he could no longer see the shapes of birds. He blinked his eyes. In the wispy, grey air, it was difficult to know if it was a girl he could see or not. Hard to tell really. He squinted. It was a girl. As he walked back he could see long hair lifting up in the heat. He was buggered if he knew where she'd sprung from though.

'Gidday,' Albert kept his hands in his pockets.

'Hello. Great fire you've got going.' She was only dressed in what looked to be a curtain. It was no wonder she was standing so close to the fire. And no shoes. Albert edged out of the smoke. Couldn't she see the burning birds?

'Feel like some soup,' he picked his thermos out of the sand. 'It's Alphabet. Vegetables and noodles.'

'No, thanks all the same,' she said. 'I've got to get going. We're camping on the headland. Only got here today.'

Albert took off his hat and stuck out his hand. 'Albert Ertle,' her hand was warm but especially her thumb. 'I'm staying at The Blue Lagoon with my brother.'

'Oh, right. You must be the guys in that tiny old van? The one with little porthole windows?'

Albert nodded.

'It's really adorable. Anyway, we'll probably see you round.'

Albert watched her moving away. He'd bet his bottom dollar she had nothing on under her curtain. Enough to freeze your butt off. In the firelight, Albert's small balding patch lit up with sweat. He'd lost his appetite for his favourite soup. It was lukewarm now and he threw it into the flames. The black lumps that were birds had fallen onto the bright coals. The red foot of a gull smouldered and spat like bacon in a frying pan. Albert stoked the fire and went off, thinking of a burning; feathers scorched and ants dying.

Albert did see the girl again — the day he decided to walk to the beach curving way in the distance to the east. It was something to do and such a nice day he'd given the pub a miss. Sidney had got involved in a snooker game and didn't enjoy walking long distances on the beach. His legs were so fat that where his thighs rubbed the skin wore away.

She was lying on a slab of rock at the fifth cove. Albert knew because he'd been counting them. Then it was better on the homeward journey because you knew how close to home you were. He stopped dead when he caught sight of her and teetered on a painful rock. His feet were tender and white. She was on her back with her hands cushioning her head. All she had on was a seashell bikini bottom. Albert's heart began pumping. He didn't dare move. Her breasts were pale brown: the colour of a favourite hen's egg. He took off his hat. He put it back on. Was the shell attached or was it just sitting on top? Albert wished she'd stand up so he could see. He wondered about the colours beneath the white shell. There would be sand grains.

She rolled over onto her front. The beach towel was bright blue, sea blue. So was the string stretching up her bottom. Albert was mesmerised. The cheeks were a deep brown with two red circles where she'd been lying. His eyes fell toward the blue ribbon. Was it a clever slip knot holding everything together?

A voice yelled 'Tas.' A man was calling. Albert's un-ravellings stopped. He turned quickly to go, his lumpy trousers sagging. He had a last look. He saw a young man with nothing on but a silver chain running towards her. But he was running towards Albert. He picked up Albert's fallen hat and smiled. He was very hairy. Tas sat up. 'Hi,' she said. Her breasts were springing like spinning tops. Albert hurried away, squashing his hat on crookedly, beyond words.

That night it was Albert's turn for the top bunk. He crawled under a blanket before Sidney was back and looked across to the dusty light globe hanging from a cord in the ceiling. Tas her name was. Or Tasman, like the sea. Or the explorer. And once he'd ridden a big chestnut winner called 'Tasman's Joy.' The roof of his mouth was raw from sucking five of Sid's boiled hum-bugs, one after the other.

Albert rolled over to face the wall, thinking about her. He felt so close he could see her pink tear ducts and the line of her eyebrows. He imagined her hot, soft thumbs were on his aching knee.

He hit the ground with a real thud. Just like a kid does in his sleep, except his bones wouldn't bend. No time to curl up and cushion the fall with his shoulder. The black and white bulls-eye shot from his mouth into the dust under the sink. Albert felt his coccyx bone cracking into three. The caravan rocked on its wheels. Shutting his eyes, Albert remembered the terrible mix up in 1961 in the Quarterman's Cup: three horses killed and his own body ground into the muddy turf; young Smitty so busted up he'd never ride again.

Albert lay sideways on the cold vinyl, waiting for Sidney. Like a storm-stunned bird, he could only flap his arms. His skin felt salty and dried. The screen door with its ripped gauze banged and groaned. Soon the mozzies would be onto him, the sand midges. He lis-tened to the sound of the van's walls contracting for the night. His legs were numbing as if buried in wet sand.

He looked up into Sidney's face as he walked through the door. Sid was so fat he couldn't have glimpsed his privates for a decade. His belly had popped out of its shirt and as Sidney bent down, Albert watched it fold into rolls of fat. He laughed when Sidney straightened. There were thick, white stripes on his brother's stomach, like a bit of fatty bacon. Even though it hurt, Albert had to laugh again. Sidney tanned in lines. The crying only began when it came to him he could hardly hear his own voice. It was fading and whimpered. His ears felt sand clogged. He could anticipate the sand pouring in and the ants.

A Wedding

Teddie watched the legs of the wedding guests sitting down all around them. He was small enough for nine not to have to crouch underneath the tables. But Meric Malley, whose father was built like a bull, was having difficulties. They were sitting back to back at the beginning of a long stretch of trestle tables, arranged in half an E-shape to the bridal table. It was taking a long time for people to reach their places. Teddie reckoned that all up, half of the district was present for his sister's wedding.

They'd taken two drumsticks of chicken in with them to help the time go while everyone sat down. But the sight of a fungus growing in Dulcie's toenails, she was sitting in front of them, put Teddie right off eating. He was sure he could smell it and gave his chicken to Meric. He saw how the black hairs of Dulcie's ankles avoided growing over the green lumps that were veins.

Their feet began to get pins and needles. Teddie could feel the tingling travelling up his left leg. He wriggled to change position. Meric sat still, staring at his big toe. It had slowly turned purple and he was wondering what would happen if it exploded. He hit his shoulder against Teddie to draw attention to it and wished he had a rubber band to put on. Then his toe would really swell up.

Teddie glared at him not to talk. It was time to move so they'd be under the top table by the time the speeches got going. Teddie led the way. It was his sister's wedding and he was going to be at that top table even if no one except Meric knew. The blue light of the plastic marquee turned their faces into patches as they moved. Meric couldn't stop giggling at the sight of Teddie on his hands and knees, the blue light on his shaved head.

'You look like a bald monkey Teddie,' Meric tried to scratch under his arms but below the trestles it was impossible and anyway, Teddie wasn't watching.

It was because Teddie's head was shaved for nits that they weren't sitting at the table. The school nurse wouldn't listen to Teddie trying to explain about the wedding. She started chopping before he'd even finished talking. And his mother had said there was no way anyone was going to be sitting at the bridal table with a lousy head.

They crawled with caution but the sharp dirt made it hard. Bits of rock kept digging into the loose skin around their knees. The smaller lumps of gravel stuck to the soft part of their hands. Meric groaned and pretended to collapse. Teddie waved a foot angrily.

'I shouldn't of brung you Meric if you don't shut up.'

Meric wasn't listening. He'd just spotted a pile of chicken bones and gristle and one piece of baked pumpkin next to what looked like old Aub's legs.

'Eh Ted. Is that old Aub?' Meric laughed softly. 'Silly old bugger must've forgot all the dogs was tied up.'

'Stupid old bugger,' echoed Teddie. The ants were already massing on the chicken skin. Meric wished the ants weren't there. He felt like a bit of baked vegetable. He was that hungry and already regretting he hadn't stayed above the tables where the food was.

'Eh Ted,' he grabbed the ankle already crawling away. 'You got anything left to eat?'

Teddie handed him some hot peanuts from his pocket. He felt as greasy as a rissole with sweat. It was hot with all these legs round and he wondered how Meric could be hungry in such conditions. Seeing Meric's long fringe flopping everywhere, almost made Teddie glad of his own hairless condition.

Betty from Busby Crossing was reached without incident. Teddie knew her by the red hemline that covered her knees. Everyone knew she only had the one good dress: bright red and worn for birthdays, christenings and Christmas. Teddie hadn't seen it at a wedding before, because this was his first wedding ever. Her feet were tapping about nervously.

'Spastic grasshopper,' hissed Teddie, pausing in front of the ankles. It was as if the red vinyl sandals had a life of their own. There were ginger hairs growing on both big toes and the legs were freckled over. Under red nail polish, black rims were still clearly visible. Teddie could picture her head bobbing away over her food.

'Silly old bat,' whispered Meric, and wished he could give her a real fright. With regret he inched past to follow Teddie. The hardest thing was getting through the slats of wood at the end of one trestle and then over and into the next. Teddie was sure Meric was going to get stuck. He thought it a miracle no toes had been trodden on yet.

They passed The Little Maggot's legs swinging above the ground. Through the trestle wood they could hear his small, shrill voice telling someone about riding his bike ten miles into school.

'That's bullshit,' muttered Teddie. 'He catches the bus with me.'

'Little turd,' said Meric.

A conversation further along the table stopped them dead. A man was saying how he wouldn't mind getting into the bridesmaid's pants. Teddie was as startled as Meric. That was Meric's sister they were talking about and she was only five years older than them. They both craned their necks to the left to try and make out who belonged to the moleskin trousers and shiny riding boots. It was hard to tell as apart from The Little Maggot, who was wearing his black school shoes, all the legs at this table had on moleskins and boots. Meric spat on his finger and drew one of his Dracula faces in the dust on the leather. He included a tongue and drops of blood. Teddie clapped silently in appreciation. He had to hand it to Meric, he had a quick mind when needed.

Their backs were beginning to ache by the time they reached the table with the six inch nails hammered through the butcher-paper table cloth. But there wasn't far to go. The nails were a landmark devised by Teddie. He'd been left the job of tacking down the paper but when he'd run out of tacks, couldn't find the Cottees jar full of short nails. There'd been no alternative to the long fencing ones, so he'd put them to good use by marking out the table next to the top one. Only now did it occur to him that someone might spike themselves. He hoped not or there'd be hell to pay from his mother. He could see her legs only a matter of yards away, her fat feet squeezing out of blue high heels. Up above, champagne corks popped. Meric's father could be heard asking where in the bloody heck Meric had got to. Teddie and Meric looked at each other, suddenly remembering they were meant to keep the drink supply going so no one could complain of getting dry during the speeches. Teddie wasn't all that worried. In his experience kegs emptied themselves and people would get the tops off beer bottles with their teeth if they had to.

Meric was close behind when they turned the corner into the final stretch. They were both covered in red dirt and even Meric's shorts were leaking sweat. Teddie put a piece of gravel in his mouth like he'd seen them do in television survival movies and made Meric do the same. Meric could only grunt. He was fed up with the whole thing. He needed a piddle and a drink. It was hotter than ever and Teddie's Dad had only begun to rave about what a good catch his new son-in-law had made.

It went on longer than even Teddie had imagined. His back was crooked and Meric looked like he'd never get up again. He'd turned over onto his belly and was supporting his head with his elbows on the ground. From the knee down, his legs poked into the air. Teddie stayed squatting in front of the bridal pair, not daring to move. There were a few big hopper ants running round. Teddie hoped none would head for Meric. A bite from one of those and nothing in the world would keep Meric quiet. Teddie noticed his sister's shoes were covered in a film of dust and wondered if he dared to wipe them clean. She'd looked so white that morning, he hated to see the red dirt. He felt for a handkerchief. Meric obliged by handing him one with only a corner crumpled by snot. But Teddie realised he couldn't do it. In fact he hardly dared breathe and wished he could do something to shut up Meric, who was panting away like any old dog.

Through the legs of the sister and new husband, Teddie and Meric could see limited frames of the outside world. They could see the old grey hills hoist going round slowly in the hot wind, with undies and towels and things still on the line. In the final rush in the morning to get to the church, they'd been forgotten. Some of the smaller kids were roaming around already. There seemed to be flocks of dirty chickens and children spreading everywhere.

The husband had mumbled his short and hard to hear speech and Pellet from the property next door was coming to the end of the telegrams.

'"Stop riding the horses and get into the curves," from Tom Babbage with best wishes.'

The last telegram was specifically for Teddie's sister, '"Take advice from one who knows. Put on your nightie and tie it to your toes," love Minnie.'

Teddie could hear the laughter but couldn't see what was so funny. Pellet was laughing too. Meric was feeling in his pocket for one of the chicken bones. His stomach was rumbling like it was going to burst.

Teddie was only feet away from the husband's hand that slipped between his sister's legs. Teddie waited expectantly for her to jab him one. He couldn't believe it. Nothing, and the hand looked shiny with chicken grease. Meric, who'd bitten the top off his chicken leg to suck out the marrow, couldn't take his eyes off the big hand that kept on exploring, even after the last telegram.

Then it was finished. People were hopping up all over the place to have a stretch and get to the beer before everybody else did. There wasn't much point in retreating the way they'd travelled. Already the lower tables had lost their rows of legs. There was no point. Teddie felt emptied of purpose. For the first time he felt the stuffiness around him. Meric was writing his name in the dirt with the remains of his drumstick. Then the feet at the top table were also treading backwards and departing. The bride shoes went last, dirtier than ever. Teddie's eyes followed their progress into the milling legs. He heard more voices of congratulations and the spitty kisses of old relations. Someone had let the rest of the chooks out and a little Lambert girl was almost strangling one, trying to pick it up. Meric disappeared. Teddie emerged last. No one had noticed them. The sunlight was sharp and outside the tent, the farm was made up of squares and triangles of light, with thin dark lines that were trees. Teddie winked his eyes. Meric was nowhere to be seen. The top of the tables were a mess, the butcher paper patterned with finger-marks of grease. The tent drooped and smelt sweaty in the afternoon heat. And Uncle Albert's mangy old kelpie was peeing on the table legs! Uncle Albert was hopping around the kegs on crutches, his ankle in a bandage from his accident. Teddie moved in to give the old dog a boot. He didn't hear his mother behind him.

'You bloody little blighter Teddie,' in one of her hands was a half eaten piece of passionfruit slice. In the other, a woollen beanie. 'You know you're meant to have this on,' she stuffed the rest of the cake into her mouth, licked her fingers, then pulled his head towards her. Teddie felt the stickiness of her fingers as she adjusted it roughly. It was the dreaded nit catcher hat. Made years ago for his elder brothers, it had stretched and was too large for Teddie's pin head. It almost reached his eyes and itched worse than the nits. 'Don't let me see it off again and don't go pestering your sister unless you want her to have the headlice on her honeymoon.'

Teddie did not want her to have the headlice on her honeymoon. He ducked away from his mother and made for the toilet. The old thunder box had been rigged up on account of the toilet inside the house being broken. Old Uncle Albert, who wasn't really related but who'd been called Uncle for as long as Teddie could remember, had been changing a light bulb in the bathroom for his mother, the week before the wedding, when he'd crashed through the lid of the toilet. Just about busted his ankle and got it stuck in the curve. The whole bowl had to be smashed up before they could get him out. His mother said it was typical of Uncle Albert not to do anything the easy way.

Teddie held his nose going through the hessian door. All that beer on such a hot day and it was no wonder it was filling quickly. It nearly made him puke but at least it kept the big blowies away from the food.

He took his hat off. Meric waltzed by with half a cream sponge in his hand. 'Seen better hair on cheese,' Meric yelled.

Teddie felt as deflated as the afternoon. There was only one place to go. Avoiding his Mum, he grabbed himself a couple of bottles of Cherry Cheer, salvaged what he could of a passionfruit slice from the flies and the sun, and headed for his water tank. He took off his shirt and squimpy tie and crawled underneath the tank-stand into the shade. He lay on his back and tipped the red drink down his throat. It didn't matter if it spilt. From very far away, he could hear lots of voices skitching and the yakking of dogs. Someone had started up a dog fight.

For a moment, Teddie propped himself up for a look. A man in a purple shirt was asleep at a table with a cigarette still in his mouth. Teddie eased himself back onto the cool, damp dirt. Meric would probably be along later. The story about dead men's nails growing out of cement graves, all curly and sharp, circled his head. He lay looking up at the water tank and the blue, dark sky. It was his favourite pastime: waiting for the drips from the tank to fall. The best part of it was you never knew where the cold water would hit. It was dripping in a pattern on his ribs now.

His mother was shrieking for him, 'Edward Arthurs, Edward Arthurs,' which must mean something because she was using his full name. But Teddie was listening to the water cleaning his wet, white, naked chest and thinking: wondering about the grown up girls at school and about a weeklong honeymoon at the Dog Creek Hotel.

Birdscarer

His paper and comb tune peeps wheezily in the afternoons. He can play one tune only and does so over and over again until his sister Elly, who is three years older, charges at him with her umbrella-tree-sword and tells him to shut up.

'Be quiet stupid Jamie Jim or I'll stab you through the heart,' and pursues him through the garden to pin him against the fence. Only when he pleads in a high voice for mercy does she release him.

I listen to them as my mother makes me stretch out my arms and stand on tip toes. The tape measure is slipping through her fingers and her mouth holds an artillery of pins. I'm to begin work immediately, as the small newspaper advertisement promised and my mother has decided to adjust the uniform provided. It's Saturday afternoon and the sweat is popping beneath her nose and spreading in patches from her breasts.

She leans towards my small bust and traps it in her tape measure. I'm wearing nothing but a bra and pants so the curtains are drawn. Orange and thick, they're soaking in the hot, late sun and turning the sewing room into a prison. I look down at my stomach. It's all orange and hot too and getting damp. My belly button is a tight coil in the middle; trapped and awful looking with the skin wrinkling into a shadowing slit. Further down, the appendicitis scar is an almost invisible diagonal. A line and a circle map my stomach and I wonder if that has any meaning at all.

From next door I hear the wild shrieks as little James Morrison falls to the ground to be tickled.

'Down on your knees, down on your knees, Silly Sir

James if you want to live. If you want to see the morning light.' His sister's voice is breathless and thin from the chase. It's easy to tell she must have Mrs Wignall for fifth class. Mad about knights and silver armour. I remember when I was in her class I was allowed to bring Punch to school for a week. After lunch Mrs Wignall would hand me a stick wrapped with silver foil and make me charge madly round yelling challenges into the air. This was meant to give everyone an idea of mediaeval jousts on horseback.

I can feel by the way my mother tugs at the material that she's getting irritable. She snaps at me, 'Keep your arms straight!' The measurements are taking ages and my arms are aching. I look again at my stomach that even in the orange curtain glow is pale because all summer I've been wearing one piece swimmers. It's an old one piece and far too small. The elastic for the legholes has had it and the legholes droop away from my thighs. But the top is so tight across my breasts they squash to show up swollen and dark when I get out of the water. This means I have to wear an extra large t-shirt over the swimmers.

I could get myself new clothes, new swimmers, my mother said brightly, when she first showed me the job ad. Somehow, that made me sadder than ever about getting work in the holidays. What's the point of having new swimmers if I'm going to be at work all the time? She said with Albert Ertle gone, there was no reason for me to be mucking round with horses anymore. She said a job would keep me out of mischief.

It's hard to believe Mr Ertle the ex-Cheesemite, is gone for good, and the horses. They were all sold. A sister came and organised everything and then a brother, to take him away. He was hurried off by his brother Sidney to Sydney the city. People reckoned Mr Ertle was going funny and that there were debts.

When I said I'd have to take a day off school to help sell the horses, my parents called me a peculiar child, but agreed.

The horses we advertised in the paper sold well, the mares and Punch. The prettier ponies though, went through a Wednesday horse sale with no reserves. Seeing them go to the dogger man must have broken the Cheesemite's heart. I sat with him on the hard wood bench of the sale ring and tried not to notice him shake as the hammer belted down the final bid on each frightened horse. Knowing he was leaving this old town had already broken his heart, the poor bugger. I looked at him once when all his horses were through and saw his eyes gone the colour of cold dishwater they were so old and sad.

I hadn't thought until then about oldness: the acid smell. How getting old meant vomit specks on the discoloured white marble round his bathroom sink. Leaving knives and forks in the fridge because of dirt and cockroaches or the dead rats still bent under the traps that the hungry cats worried over. Once Mr Ertle left, I remembered things like that or how I'd gone round to the house and found a pool of sour yellow oil soaking into the wood of the kitchen table. It was one of the six-pound slabs of butter that he used to get from his old dairy connections. The bread and crusts from his sandwiches were deep in the oily flood. Last summer was a stinker and it knocked the stuffing out of him, though I didn't see it then. I remember making a big joke about the butter.

The chant of the Morrison children is a happy chant through the windows. They are singing a song about snails. Garden snails the colour of pink and grey mist that are crushed underfoot on footpaths. Then the children are silent and I hear their determined feet on their own garden path, looking for snails. 'For a snail race,' yells James.

Or when they grow bored, perhaps they'll mash them with bare feet or peel off the brown thin shells, cracking them first against any hard surface like an egg against the rim of an eggcup.

I ate two boiled eggs the day of Mr Ertle's departure. It was the end of term Maths test and I didn't see him go. The test was the reason for the eggs. My mother believes that next to meat, eggs are the great fortifiers and she was insistent. So all through the algebra and formulas, I silently burped the taste of egg and silver teaspoon and thought of the departure I'd never see.

I said I'd write and probably I will. I have the address, a dull sounding flat number in a street and suburb I've never heard of. Or maybe I never will write for I wonder how I'd ever begin. 'Dear Mr Ertle,' or 'Dear Albert,' or 'Dear Cheesemite — this is what I used to call you though I never told you or anyone that.'

And there's the problem of how to end. Whether or not to sign off with 'love from,' or 'lots of love from,' or just 'all the best.'

Already the For Sale sign on his leaning gate has fallen flat. The grass and weeds are growing. To me it's a lifeless house now. A while back I went and looked through the kitchen windows dead with thick cobwebs. There were potatoes scattered across the floor all wrinkling green and shooting in twists. They must have been overlooked in the move — the sack of potatoes that were always kept in the darkness behind the kitchen door. Probably rats had tipped them over but it was as though they'd moved across the lino themselves and were crouching — ready to explode with a bad, black smell and a final decay.

All along the verandahs, the shutters are closed so I've never seen what's left in any of the other rooms. I imagine other vegetable forms of life are taking over: creepers inching through the floor boards and going wild in the cool, low ceilinged rooms.

My mother is telling me to watch how she manages the temperamental sewing machine but what I'm seeing is the empty line of stables. There was a deep rot in the timber before Mr Ertle left. Where the paint was missing I could rub the soft wood away with my fingernail. It was bruised and pale like his face that I kissed goodbye. Awkward. I kissed his cheek and my lips went into the soft sinking flesh. I smelt disinfectant like the yellow deodorant discs used to cover up the pong of old toilets. His collapsing mouth touched my chin. The lips were gummy. On his death certificate they'll put 'Decay of Nature' as the cause of death and they'll be correct. It's not right that he's been taken away. He should've been allowed to decay in his own house where he's been for so long. The house he grew up in, went away from and came back to. It was a farmhouse. Once, before the town encroached into the paddocks, streets dividing the land and the big family scattering, Mr Ertle the Cheesemite grew up. He had a heap of sisters and only the one brother. Sometimes he told me names but they slid from my mind. It's easy to forget if you've never met the people. Lots of them are dead anyway. A while back, all Mr Ertle seemed to be doing was going to the funerals of his dead family. Some were in different states and he'd come back tired and absent minded. I remember stories better. Only his sister Adelaine married a dairy farmer — the only one to end up on a dairy farm. Mr Ertle said his father wouldn't have believed it, not after the endless milking they'd taken turns with. Only because he began to do no good as a jockey — too old, too heavy, did Mr Ertle move back. A fair bit of the land had already gone and he sold most of the rest, to live on the money he made. With dairying the way it is now, automated, swift and unprofitable for small farms, it's just as well he didn't try to make a go of it. Still, it must've been funny to look out from the verandah he was a small boy on, and see the brick and fibro houses, most of the trees chopped down. All up, there were nine Ertles or ten I think.

Now everything is deserted. It is a deserted house straight from the dark, crowded print of a fairy tale except the walls are old weatherboard. And twice haunted. By the even skinnier girl that was me a few summers ago; before Mr Ertle broke his coccyx and then his ankle and went downhill from there. And by the big and noisy family I can never know; faces in a faded family photograph.

'Try this for size,' says my mother. She's panting heavily in the small room from the heat and the exertion. Even a thing like using her old Singer, gets her puffed. It would be good to be swimming a horse down at The Spit. Or rummaging through Mr Ertle's old garden looking in the undergrowth for cool fallen mangoes the flying foxes had missed. It's a giant garden, full of fruit trees and other remnants of a past existence; farm gates almost invisible under the chokos, wooden sulky traces almost part of the earth. But being an obedient daughter I don't try to resist the polyester cotton uniform going down over my head. It feels tight where she's sewed two big darts into the bustline but she says it's good.

Looking in the mirror though, for she's urged me to admire her skill, I see that I look like a scarecrow. A bright yellow Bird Scarer and I flap my arms accordingly. I mean to disrupt the oppression but instead draw attention to the hemline. 'Too long,' she declares so that I feel trapped in her airless little sewing room and long to scream and yelp as James and Elly Morrison next door are doing. They are such a happy pair of children our new neighbours have. They moved next door after Mrs Humberstone was put into a home. They like to make a lot of noise and they've put in an above ground swimming pool plonk on the place where Mrs Humberstone grew her stocks and marigolds. The children have changed the landscape of this street with their games. And in the air, tennis balls hang lost on string wrapped around the telegraph wires.

Through a crack in the curtains I see the pool water with a collection of leaves and twigs floating in the middle. James and his sister have the right idea for a hot afternoon like this. They're not in the pool yet but have stripped down to their undies to be cold under the sprinkler. As the sewing machine clackers away, I watch the rusty arms of the sprinkler turn around, the wet and running bodies of children. Then they move the sprinkler and are capering out of sight.

The thin silver needle going in and out of the yellow cloth reminds me of an old nightmare that would send me running into the big double bed. It was safe then between the two warm bodies that were my parents. They lay either side of me and made my dreams go quiet inside. My mother soft and overflowing like a pudding; my father all knobs and angles but so warm there inside his big shoulder blades. Whichever way I turned, I felt safe. Even thinking back to the needle glinting nightmare, I could feel secure. It was my triumph over any horrible dream. But when I was bigger and came snuffling in, Dad would groan and then leave the room for my small bed. The empty left hand side was a gap I couldn't fill and my nightmare would return sharper than before and more terrifying without that bony back there to lean my body against.

In the morning I'd pass my bedroom and see him stretched out, his long legs burst through the tucked in sheets and drooping a foot over the end of the bed. No matter how busting I was to reach the toilet, I'd stop for a look. For he slept with the whites of his eyes showing and a thin loop of hairy bottom.

The noise of the sewing stops and I watch my mother snip through the tangle of cotton. She tells me to switch on the iron so the new hemline can be flattened. It's meant to show exactly the right amount of thigh but it looks too short. Still, I go over and give her a bit of a hug because I know she's tried hard. Outside I can hear the Morrison children have abandoned the hose and sprinkler for the swimming pool. I pull back the curtain to see what's making them laugh so much. They've blindfolded each other with their pants and are churning

102

through the water. James is snorting water and screech-ing about making a whirlpool. Suddenly they've stopped running and it's quiet — the water swirling around silently with a current strong enough to pull their brown bodies in a circle.

My mother snaps the curtain across sharply and tells me to get away from the window in my underwear. I'm swallowing down hard because I feel like crying. Like the bright circling bodies I'm caught in a current. I can't pull out because my parents keep prodding me back. Being made to work reminds me of early swimming lessons at the municipal baths. A bossy voice telling me to put my arms out straight and kick, kick, kick with my head under water until I touched the other side. Be-cause I couldn't open my eyes under water I'd struggle through the bubbling dark in a crooked spiral.

It will be a horrible job, working with meat and chip oil and truckies from the long roads west. I'm a vegetarian now, much to my mother's disgust. She's a Meat Believ-er. Three meaty meals a day — sausages, chops, steak, kidney and all other sorts of vital organs from sheep, cattle and pigs — were dished up to my father for twenty years at least. Since Dad's operation though, she's been hacking the fat from the lumps of meat she loves to fry up. Doctor's orders. I sense her reluctance. The meat is all mottled where the flesh has bruised during slaughter. Purple and brown splotches spread out from the pearly sheen of muscle. I think of Dad all opened up on the operating table and have to turn away. Hopefully hamburger mince won't be so bad. It will only be pulped meat, kept red and white by edible preservatives. Nothing could be worse than lambs fry. The liver of lambs floating in the stainless steel sink of my mother's kitchen. I've abandoned the job she once set me of peeling the livers. Slipping in the sharp knife and making the brown flat ovals pop from the skin.

The odours of meat, any meat, hang in my nose like

the smell of a dead animal hidden from the road. It makes me ill. My mother says I'll never fatten up on oranges. 'Sausages!' proclaims the Meat Believer my mother. 'Have a sausage. You can't not eat sausages at a sausage sizzle!' But they are worse still, containing the remains of horses hooves, intestines and worse. I won't think of the blood on the lamb white wool, the blood on aprons of bearded men, smeared over the cheeks of women in the freezing rooms who cut and pack. The school excursion to the meatworks was a mistake. I cut my thumb on the sharp paper of my exercise book. A horde of flies landed and I watched my thumb bleed and change shape with the eager, light weight bodies. Like black crows on dying livestock they couldn't be shaken off.

I miss Mr Ertle the old Cheesemite. I miss his creamy yellow milk, seeing him skim the black dots from a freshly milked bucket and pouring it into our strong black tea. It's ages now since I've had anything except milk from a bottle. I'm scared I wouldn't like the taste of real milk anymore, the stronger flavour warm in my mouth. Mr Ertle would be disappointed with me. For the old favourite cow he gave me was sold. A great, great grandchild of his father's favourite milker, he liked to believe. She fetched a good price but that didn't lift away my guilt. My mother said it was dangerous for my father to have runny green mud where he might slip.

The air is breathless, floating with dust. The fine lint particles of the sewing room sift before my eyes in the sun through the window. It's time for the final fitting. I feel my mother's hands hot on me from the ironing of the hem as she turns me again to the full length mirror. I stare not at my reflection but at the dirt blotches held captive beyond the glass. I'm a bright yellow line down the middle. I see that if I bend over my pants must show and any skinny white bottom escaping from the elastic.

The zipper that fastens me at the front chops my body vertically in half and won't slide far enough up. I see that from both ends I'll be vulnerable to the eyes behind the counter. Perhaps it'll be a high counter though and they won't matter so much — my small breasts that tilt at the zip-end, this naked hem line.

Slowly I become aware of my mother standing angrily, a fat watcher by the window. She's indignant and heavily perspiring as the sun catches her face through the glass. The Morrison children are still in the nud but have left the water — tadpoles into hoppers. They've scaled the blue bending sides of the pool and are clinging by their toes to the narrow plastic edging. Their arms are out and waving erratically to keep balance. They are as brown and polished as well used leather. Their fingers and feet twitch and dance as if controlled by the strings of sunlight falling down. Lying on the bindi eye lawn is their fallen underwear. They're flung, blue, green and red, bright in some careless pattern.

At some stage Mrs Morrison must have brought them refreshments for their mouths are sucking at the long cordial icypoles in plastic tubes. Like anxious birds they tilt their thin necks back to sip at the frozen sweetness. And all the time wobbling crazy round the edge of the pool.

They catch sight of me looking across and I wave with both hands at them in silent applause. I see that I've gone and startled them. They pause and teeter, their arms outstretched and flapping. Then they are under the water making urgent sign and bubble language I cannot read. I am full of tears, a frightening yellow figure to children playing games. And this time it's me not my mother pulling the curtains shut.

The Midnight Shift

He hurts her with his eyes shut and his tongue poked out and the smell of hamburgers still on his fingers. Two Big Boy Special Burgers with the Lot, double cheese and sauce but no beetroot. I know exactly, because it's either me or Vorna who gets them ready. Sometimes when ordering, he'll say that just for something different I can make it hot dogs with yellow mustard. It is nothing new for him to have two cartons of chips along with a chocolate malted thickshake. No wonder he is such a shape. Like a Huntsman spider with a swollen belly. And all day clinging over a power drive steering wheel with the vinyl seating getting hot in the afternoon sun.

She tries not to touch the moles that are spongy on his shoulders. Some have hairs growing out the middle. She watches them while he grunts, and the sweat that beads along his skin. Once a piece of earwax fell out. It rolled down her face like a tear.

His neck is bull red and I think that if she only dared to bite that throbbing vein he would die. The blood would spurt high in the air and pattern her skies more brilliant than any sunset.

Standing behind the front counter I can see the sunsets. Between busloads of hamburger eaters I watch them spatter, streak, light up, glow yellow, look like jam or flower colours, go smokey, go gold, go mauve, Go Shell. Go Well With Shell. Across the highway, the other service station interupts my view. It is a decrepit building that sprawls in dim oblong shapes by the side of the road, but the Shell sign is always lighted by dusk. Five minutes before Mulvy Smith who runs this place

106

switches on our Golden Fleece ram. For a while after I started work at the Roadhouse I tried to think of original ways to see the sun through the falling clouds. The same way I used to learn a new word from the dictionary every day. Like my attempts to improve my vocabulary, all efforts have faded. My mind overloads with other people's sunset descriptions and the smell of chips in their boiling vats.

By sundown Vorna, who arranges the salads for the sit-down people, is telling me about her aunt who has been in the nursing home for donkeys years.

'Those chips ready to go love?' she asks, making the rolls of Kraft-sliced stand straight in rings of tinned pineapple. 'It's a crying shame,' she is slicing the buttered bread into triangles. The crusts are only a bit stale. 'For all those years she's just a little Bean. A vegetable, you know. And now after all this they decide to operate. Diviticulitis it was. Got to wear a bag now. A Colostomy.' Vorna finds the word she is looking for and spills grease from a chiko roll down her yellow zippered uniform. It coagulates in the metal teeth as the rest of the night passes.

Above the floor that gets slimy with fallen foods, above the two garbage bins filling with multi-colouring pig slops, higher than the washing up sinks and the clock, is a strip of glass. Suns only set in the west when I'm out the front and serving at the counter. In the kitchen all I can see are the trains going past. First comes the cold chrome clanking as they slow down at the edge of the town lights. Through the high thin window I see the wooden overpass bridge bending and shaking. It seems that the bridge is right above the kitchen. I imagine disasters. Falling passengers scattering the trays of buns I butter. People splashing into the egg and milk mix the floured cutlets have to be dunked into. Sleeping babies in bunny rugs screaming awake as they crash land in the chocolate sauce bucket.

The air is lonelier after the train noises die. The night

shift is the sad shift. The sound of the swings outside in the empty picnic area gives me the shivers. Vorna drops Winfield 25 ash into burgers and the other counter girl goes home. My banana thickshake dinner tastes of chemicals. I eat cold chips one by one to disguise the taste. Vorna drops a whole butt on top of a steak and egg sandwich and covers it in a pool of barbeque sauce. Maybe I know nothing at all and Vorna is out to sabotage the popularity of Mulvy and Dougie Smiths famous roadhouse big-boy-burgers, that are even being advertised on the radio. Anything's possible I suppose, at that time of night when the truckies begin to come in. Hearing truck gears changing in the night is a faraway feeling. The groaning of brakes as they pull in turns my insides cold. From the kitchen I can hear Vorna with the radio on listening to the dogs. She never misses a bet on a Friday night. Doors slam; boots hit the tar. Gravel crunches.

Trucks heading north come to this servo. Trucks going South normally pull up at the Shell one across the road. South going trucks with drivers wanting a screw make the effort to swing across the highway and come here. There are more of these last sort of driver than I ever would have imagined. They come through the door smelling of diesel and dust. They wear little caps and tatooes on their arms and T-shirts like I often sell, with something dirty on the front. Sometimes they go straight on upstairs while Vorna gets their meals ready. They go outside and round the back to get to the stairs. I hear them creaking up the slat and air steps and then the doors shutting.

That is not always his way of doing things. Often he'll eat chips and one burger first of all.

She knows when he arrives. She can smell the cattle in four long layers moaning on the truck.

Tonight one steer with horns has got its head stuck between the rails and bellows crookedly into the night. From behind the gauze curtain that shifts with the hot

108

air, she watches the headlights snap off. As she lies on the bed she feels her heart curl inside her.

Vorna says they are King size with satin black covers and red canopies and all but I don't know. Vorna can't but help let her imagination go when it comes to the women upstairs. Vorna says there are girls who park panel vans in the By-Pass Rest area and wait for truckies there. Which isn't so hard to believe.

I have a memory of the first time I saw him. It was in my first week of work when I was trying to get the hang of things in a hurry. He wanted chips before he went upstairs. I scooped out two small scuttleloads. They were the remnants from the chip-display-unit; chip fragments rather than chips and some bits burnt. They barely filled the carton let alone spilled over like the photo-ads above the counter show. But I was tired and just about to clean the chip display glass. To do this you have to put your head and shoulders right inside the glass doors and angle the spray bottle into the greasy corners. I could see him through the tinted glass flipping over the box full of country and western cassettes and shovelling the chips into his mouth. He came across and pressed his face up against the glass. I could see the hairs out his nose and the chips hanging onto his calcified and jagged eye teeth. And white skin the texture of bloater tripe or frozen potato. He smiled through the glass. I made him more chips because he said the others were all dried out. I had to use detergent where his nose had been.

I am all dried out, she thinks, lying on her bed upstairs. She has tried to fill the stretch marks near her hips with vaseline and baby powder. Her ears ache with listening for the footsteps on the stairs so she unscrews her bluebird earrings and sends them flying. I hear them skitter across the floor above my head as I turn out frytol tins of frozen mince into plastic tubs and into small circles with my hands. He is still eating his chips; watching the television in the corner. The meat catches under my fingernails. It has turned green and grey at the edges of the tins. It looks poisonous under the fluorescence. The colour of hail in storm clouds. The colour of the varicose veins Vorna is going to have stripped from her legs when she saves up enough holiday time. They grow like dark vines below the skin because of standing for nine hours on hard tile floors.

People should get paid more for working after twelve. The midnight shift. For every hour I get $3.52, the same rate as daytime when all you're serving is hordes of little kids on their way home from the beach. The worst they can do is not make up their minds whether to have a lemonade Icypole or a raspberry one, while the queue behind them grows longer and longer. Mothers with great welts on their shoulders from squashing their bosoms up with heavily elasticised swimmers buy suntan lotion to ease their stinging skins. They mop up spilt milkshakes with Kleenex and get annoyed when they realise they've been sitting on a bit of squashed pie. The pinballs are all whizzing so loud that I can't hear the silence upstairs. No-one's there. No-one's upstairs until late afternoon and never yet have I seen the women arrive. I only notice the three cars after the Coach tours have gone on their way to the Gold Coast, their seats full of determined purple-waved passengers. The cars are parked out the back. I see them when I go to light the incinerator.

The Ford station wagon with the bashed headlight is hers. There are kids toys on the back seat, spilt twisties, sweet packets, a baby restraint, an exercise book with a picture of a kitten pasted on brown paper and plastic covered. One day I will see her down the street on a Saturday morning lugging the shopping and the baby, and buying brown paper and pens at the Stationers for

110

her kids' first day back at school. I'll know who she is. I will know and I'll give her a friendly smile. I think it's wonderful she can think still of getting proper brown paper for her kids. When I was in Primary my Mum would never buy me brown paper or plastic to cover my books. I can remember having to wait until everyone had left the classroom before I handed my book up. A waste of time and money Mum would say but she never knew what it felt like going to school with your books covered in yellow contact meant for lining drawers. A dreadful and mortifying feeling. One year I became so desperate that I used brown bags from the butchers. Only after I'd covered my Composition book did I realise there were smears of drying blood all down one side. Funny the things that worry you at that age but it would be good to have an understanding mother.

Sometimes there is a lull in people who want to eat hamburgers and I read the paperbacks from the revolving stand out the front. They have trashy covers and are full of sex. There are the truck magazines too. There is an ad for this servo in the December issue. 'Girls for Stud Rams,' it reads and the lettering is gold and black.

In between late night truckie orders, Vorna reads me the stars. Not the night stars, The Saucepan or the Southern Cross that the Cheesemite taught me how to work out the northern direction from, but the horoscopes from her magazines. It's all such bulldust but Vorna is a horoscope addict. I am a crab–moon person linked to the water. Vorna reads that I am whimsical, wayward and a child forever. Vorna is always looking for romance. She seeks it in the to-be-continued-next week stories, between pages of Tampax ads and Royal features. It makes her feel kind sending her magazines upstairs when she's finished with them. Minus the potato cooking supplement, or is it turkey this week?

One potato, two potato, three potato four. He throbs with the rhythm of little boys playing games. *Five potato, six potato, seven potato MORE.* He has eaten his chips and gone up the stairs. The door has shut and it's only him and her alone in the room.

Slut he calls her, pulling off his boots and smelling his sweaty feet. She has had everything taken out in an operation but not her ovaries. She feels them bruising, feels them hurt and squash.

Insects are self destructing over the kitchen doorway as I cut the day-after-tomorrow's onions. It is one hour into Christmas Eve. The day before Christmas and all round the house not a creature was stirring not even a mouse. It doesn't feel like Christmas this year. I suppose because this is the first time I've ever worked in my holidays. God Arrest You Merry Gentleman. Truckies buy under-the-counter magazines and stuffed kiddies toys and sandlewood perfume and powder sets for under ten dollars. They always leave the screen door open and let the insects in. Night-time insects are different from the hot blundering flies of the day; more desperate to die. The purple-lighted insect ring screwed above the kitchen doorway gets them but not quickly. Sometimes their deaths seem to go on forever. Like the onion rings I must chop. Like the noises upstairs that are so loud and long. It's a wonder Vorna can stand there reading as she whacks eggs on the hotplate for his after-fuck burgers.

I slice the onions. The mattress is wheezing. He has streaked her skin with his oily fingernails, making her turn over like a spider moving in on a stung moth, he goes for her mouth, rearranges it, sucks and spits; leaves white thumbprints on her breasts. That's against her rules but he is determined. It's Christmas time, he groans, as if that explains everything. There is a strong smell of cow shit but whether it's coming through the window or clings to his body she can't tell.

112

Vorna is deep in her story. Her hand flips the eggs from habit. She holds the magazine close to her face because her glasses steam up over the hotplate. I cry onion tears. It is Christmas Eve and still I can't go home until these last burgers are eaten and paid for, the hotplate cleaned, the milkshake stirrers washed. My eyes weep. Vorna yelps like a kelpie that there's a man at the front waiting to be served. It is only Winding Windows, the funeral director who lives down the road from me. He mumbles hello, not expecting to see me here. He rubs his grey, greasy hair and makes up his mind to have a soft serve cone dipped in chocolate. It is one o'clock in the morning. As I dip the icecream into the container of chocolate sauce it falls off its cone. I put it back on. He trundles out licking chocolate off his nose. He must be on his way home from picking up an out-of-town corpse. The ads he puts in the paper make a point of emphasising that distance is no problem for a Battersly Burial. 'If you don't choose a Battersly Burial — it's Your funeral.' I am not at all surprised that he would finish driving home a corpse with an icecream in one hand. He owns a giant refrigerator for bodies. This is also where he keeps the beer. He drinks straight from the can. He has two shining black cars each with the most up-to-date automatic features — windows that work on a button.

Winding Windows comes back in and says his ice-cream tastes of onions. I replace it with a chiko roll. Merry Christmas he says and drives off in his hearse.

Vorna tells me to finish with the onions and go on home. Her face is heavy with old makeup. At least it is a holiday tomorrow. It's hard not to yawn. The stairs when I go outside are as empty as the road and carpark. His truck, her car, my old ute and Mulvy's are the only vehicles left. Sometime not so long ago the other two women from upstairs have gone home. Maybe they followed Winding Windows into town. The cattle in the truck are peaceful and smell rich and sweet. They don't know the abattoirs are only four miles away.

Mulvy is doing something with the garbage, waiting for Vorna, to give her a lift home. I see his teeth smiling as he says there'll be a Christmas bonus on Boxing Day. I say goodnight. Probably it'll be a free hamburger.

'Sweet dreams dear,' Vorna puts her head out the kitchen door to say goodnight. I wave and Vorna waves back, and the wild shadows on the curtains. But it is over now. There is a stillness. The moon is bony, new, fragile, thin like a toenail shot into the sky by a blunt pair of clippers. I drive slowly round to the front to reach the road. The yellow Ram and the yellow Shell shine across the highway at each other. It will be a dull dawn, a dun coloured sky.

She lies naked on the bed while he pulls his belt underneath his belly and burps. Downstairs Vorna is putting his hamburgers into a takeaway bag for him.

Sperm sticking her thighs together feels like the thick Clag glue so good for Christmas decorations. The yellow signs look to her like the shapes her children carve out of flaky school soap for her to wash her body with. Because they know she works at the Golden Fleece servo, they have made her a yellow soap ram as a special parcel to hang amongst the tinsel and pine needles. They cannot know that she will burst into tears sitting underneath the Christmas streamers when she opens their present.

He is leaving the room now. The door opens and shuts. I see him come down the stairs, a dark blob with bowing legs. A gob of spit hits the ground. He's left a packet of Drum behind and a half smoked rollie stuck to the wall above the bedhead. It glows in the grey room. She watches it burning and the bleep of the trucks red tail lights curving away.

I toot my horn. I give the engine a bit more choke to stop it stalling. It's time to go home.

114

Flat ¼

There was a small tree at the bottom left of the page, a
weeping willow with bright crayon flowers drawn
between the leaves. Albert's hand drifted from his letter
to the cold cup of tea. He drank it anyway but was
disgusted to see a last bite of sugared biscuit breaking
apart on the bottom. He couldn't remember dunking it
in. He sucked his lips to stop them quivering.

Beryl in the flat upstairs was going to the toilet. A
loud pisser old Beryl and always on time. He'd take a
bet on five minutes before the 6 o'clock news, give or
take a few seconds. He turned the television on and put
the volume up for the benefit of his birds who were
housed in a cage to the right of the kitchen. It was the
third Wednesday of the month and time again for the
Body Corporate of the flats to meet. Beryl was secretary,
self appointed so long ago, Majella said, no one remembered it was meant to be a rotational position. The
sound of her on the toilet was trickling off a bit now and
Albert sighed. Beryl Ruby bloody Rabbit. Albert was
sure she was having him on when she'd first introduced
herself. He'd hardly been moved in, before she'd come
barging through his bedroom door to say hello. He'd
never heard of such a name. But looking at her closely
as she said what a kind brother he had, he'd thought
that it suited her nicely. Her eyes leaked just like she
had the myxo.

The knock came on the door. Briefly, Albert wondered if he could fake a sickie. He imagined diving
under a chair like the cat in his favourite mouse and cat
cartoons. Too late: she was through the door and ad-
vancing towards him.

'Now then Mr Ertle,' her high vinyl heels crunched

115

bird seed into the carpet as she moved in. 'This is an important meeting. Our half yearly and we want someone there from every unit.'

'Rightyo Beryl,' said Albert. 'Righto you old witch,' he thought, at the same time bitterly wishing he'd covered up the new budgie cage. She'd moved past him to stare at it. Really, it was a small aviary, made out of the timber frame of an old black and white television. Someone had pitched it out in the last Council Clean Up and Albert moved fast to retrieve it. Getting the insides out had been a job and a half. He'd been itching to get a few more birds to breed, ever since Majella relented and said he could. The budgies were only bought the other day but seemed to be settling nicely.

Albert shuffled. 'What do you think then Beryl? Not such a bad job?' He moved across to stroke the timber. 'It's good wood.'

Beryl didn't speak so he tried for a laugh. 'Just so long as the birds don't go getting any ideas about turning into celebrities. Comedians or something.'

'You know it's against the regulations, don't you,' Beryl was circling the cage as if it was diseased. 'Poor Majella and Sid. You'll ruin their carpet. It'll have to be brought up at the meeting. A question of hygiene Mr Ertle. Lice.'

'Not my birds,' Albert was shocked. 'Oh, no, no louse on my birds. You've made a mistake there.'

But Beryl wasn't listening. She was handing Albert his hat. He placed it on his head slowly and followed her out the door. He couldn't stop his head wagging as they climbed the stairs. It was so tiring. Just about everyone had arrived by the time they reached the top. Bubbles of sweat gathered along Beryl's top lip and around the black hairs. Albert thought she must shave her moustache and the thought of her lathering up each morning made him laugh.

The meeting began with the usual rituals. Beryl Ruby Rabbit led with the treasury report and a review of the years activities to date. Albert was in the back row, half way behind a giant indoor cactus. It was a position regretted immediately. Beryl's National 100 air conditioner, one month old, was on full blast and unpleasant side winds made the hairs on his arms stand up with cold. And about every minute an extra powerful gush of air would get in under his hat. By the time the argument about what colour to repaint the balconies started up, Albert had stopped listening. Now his socks had fallen down and he felt the draughts. He crossed his ankles and took a letter from his pocket.

Dear Mr Ertle , it began
I will miss you when I go to live in Twee Heads
I have always

Albert looked up guiltily. His hearing aid had begun to peep thinly and he felt the whole room must be looking. He swatted the little knob, his body tense with the moment. In his heart he knew it was all the tall buildings affecting his ears. It stopped, and after a suitable time of looking attentive, he continued to read.

I have always known you but now I have to go. But I will remember you
LOVE from
Jessica Gilson

Albert's head shook sadly. The Gilsons had moved out a week ago and the letter arrived on Tuesday. Gil-

117

son's place was the only house left in the street with the only real garden in the area as far as Albert was concerned. The Council was always having to lop off branches from the big camphorlaurels that tangled around the electricity wires. The grass had bindies and the paths were slippery in the rain with moss. A long time ago, Sidney said, in the fifties, the street had been bulldozed away and the new red brick flats put up. They blocked the sun and made Gilson's house look out of place. The house made Albert remember the old homes on North Coast dairy farms.

In summer the western sun heated up the bricks of Sid and Majella's flat. Wetting the outside walls was the only way he knew of reducing the temperature. He was hosing his feet down with the hot water that had been sitting in the hose all day when Jessica first poked her head over the fence. She'd climbed into the wattle tree and was eating a green cordial icypole. She'd shown him how to suck the colour from the ice to make her tongue turn green. He'd met her kitten and showed her his birds. He remembered her excited shriek on seeing old Louie, his wall eyed budgie. 'Your bird wunked at me. He wunk!'

Albert's mind floated weightless in Beryl's air conditioned air. Almost asleep, his throat coughed up a lump of phlegm to work round with his tongue. He'd forgotten all about Beryl's threat to his birds. A familiar tune was starting in his head and he imagined playing it with grass and thumbs. Once he'd shown Jessica how to do it but the grass tickled her lips so much she couldn't stop laughing.

Albert slept alone in his tune as the meeting gathered force round him. They had taken the vote on cream paint versus white to re-do the railings and had moved on to other matters. The middle aged couple from Number 8 were starting to argue with each other about the wisdom of cement borders around the recently planted palms and had to be called to order by Beryl. Someone suggested it was time for a cup of tea but Beryl was already propelling the meeting on.

Albert woke suddenly to hear them discussing his grey metal garbage bin. They wanted it replaced. He was shocked. The bin was one of the few things Sidney allowed him to bring with him. Albert tried to speak but was too dry. A cup of tea would be good. He licked his lips and munched to get some spit back. It was unbelievable but one woman had just suggested they purchase a purple plastic one out of petty cash. Heads were nodding agreement! Albert was so upset he let himself out without a word. Angrily, he headed down the stairs. By cripeys he'd see about any purple pansy garbage bin. But he wished Majella and Sidney would come back from their Queensland holiday, where they were staying on a gold coast, so they said. It sounded rich and glittered in his thoughts of them.

He reached the bottom of the stairs at last and made for the garbage bin shelter. His bin looked distinctive, its lower half a darker grey where flood waters had reached it in the olden times. He put his hands around each handle and tried to jerk it into the air. Bloody heavy. He had to admit the old thing was bloody heavy. He couldn't lift it and dragged the bin instead, ignoring his heart beating too fast and the faces appearing at Beryl's window. A black scratch followed him across the concrete. He paused at the entrance into the units, panting with dislike at a row of tube cacti either side of the pine chip garden. He felt like booting them over they were so ugly.

Halfway to his door, half a week's garbage and bird seed spilled out down the stairs. Albert didn't stop except to replace the lid. He'd fix it all later. Hopefully, that flipping old shitter Beryl would land flat on her face in the potato peelings. This thought spurred him on to reach his door, get the bin inside, lock up and fall into the nearest chair. He felt his arms feeble with sweat

119

where the muscles should have been and was reminded of the damp plummage of birds washed up after storms at sea.

The sound of his budgies enjoying the theme music to the end of the news, cheered him. There was nothing they liked better than the orchestral music. After a while he walked over to them for a chat. He apologised for not staying at the meeting to defend their new house and gave them fresh seed and water. He told them everything was going to be alright. There was disbelief in his hands.

For a time he stood looking out of the front window. There was nothing to see. As far as Albert looked, lights were going on in brick blocked flats. Somewhere a car alarm was hooting. Directly opposite was a block identical in size and layout to Sidney and Majella's. A box of eight boxes in four layers, only the bricks were yellow not red. On the second level a woman in bowling whites was unpegging bras and beige corsets from a clothes horse on the balcony. On the second level next door, a younger woman was hanging out blue jeans. The two women were divided only by a one brick wall, but couldn't see each other. They went inside at the same moment and flipped their venetian blinds shut in unison. Albert wondered about that, until his gaze was caught by the curving fall of a back making love. He could see the brown skin along the backbone. Through the frame of the partly pulled curtain, he caught a glimpse of brown hair before a pair of locked shoulders rolled out of sight.

There was no sign of movement from the top level but one of the garages facing Albert opened up from the inside. It was an Asian man and his small daughter. Amongst piles of neatly stacked boxes was a small piano. She began to play while her father stacked the boxes higher around her.

The only house to be seen was the Gilson's, its roof flaking mauve in the approaching night. Albert felt his knees aching and his throat. Someone had told him that fifty years ago the area was all small farms with a few houses. He found this hard to believe. He hoped Jessica's new house in Tweed Heads would have a good supply of climbing trees. He thought of the hairy grubs that used to sting. Memories passed through him of all the trunks he'd climbed, of all the children he'd known and been.

It occurred to him that he should try and butter-up Beryl Ruby Rabbit, get her on side about the birds. Maybe he'd give her a baby budgie if the first lot hatched alright.

Albert went inside to boil himself an egg — soft boiled so he could dip his favourite burnt-toast soldier men into the shell. From the big yellow and red container of Saxa table salt, he carefully poured a small pile of salt, making sure the opening was adjusted for just the right amount.

He ate his egg quickly so it didn't get cold, in his dressing gown, in bed. It was early, he knew, but someone, he guessed Beryl, had lit the incerator and the smoke billowed across and hit his windows. There was no reason to stay up. But for a while Albert remained awake in bed staring at the deep crack in his ceiling and imagining the layers of rooms above. He wondered if everyone else's beds were in exactly the same position as his. He thought as much because he'd taken a lot of care in finding where the only bit of morning sun came in. That was why he slept with his curtains open — to get the greatest benefit of warmth before it left the flat completely.

Sidney and Majella were on a golden coast, their postcard said. *Bum Titty Bum, we're having fun.* There were three naked women pictured with yellow hair and the embossed lettering of the card was also gold.

Beryl was having a shower upstairs but Albert thought it was rain. He felt glad the incinerator would be put out and hoped the fall would be heavy enough to do the job properly. In his head the rain shivered and plopped in puddles along the road. He could hear the gutters beginning to fill and wondered if frog season had arrived.

Albert sank deeper into the lump in the middle of his mattress. It was a pity Jessica had gone before the frogs. He could have shown her how to catch the tadpoles. No one could beat his method and he could even tell which ones would most likely turn into toads. He went to sleep listening for the croaking to start, with egg yolk on his chin and an old rhyme about an old man without his head going in and out of his thoughts. He tried to catch the sound of Jessica's voice. He could hear the sing song chant but kept on missing the words. Something about the rain. Albert's head felt like cardboard. In sleep, his arm pulled the pillow over his head.

Looping the Loop

For a while he was jealous of his son on her breast. He tried to suckle her after a sprint race at the veledrome and a late night home. Then he spewed when her warm sweet milk curdled all the beer inside. After a month, he began to say:

'This tit feeding's got to stop.'

'People will get the wrong idea.'

'Think you're a trollop, a hooer, a tart, popping your boobs out at them.'

'It's unnatural.'

'Not like you to be a show-off.'

His mate Dean had a kid the same age and it was bottle fed:

'Thriving on it.'

'Couldn't get enough.'

'Not a wimp.'

'Above average weight.'

'A little man.'

'Do you want to spoil him on the titty?'

She remembers her husband's words, their slurred noise through her head after the Friday night out with the boys; the order soon afterwards to see Dean's wife about the name of the tablet she was using to dry herself up.

His voice is an endless echo in her memory. She is bitter, resigned, indifferent. Soon she will leave him. But the past is dogged. Cleaning the toilet makes her memory dredge things up.

'You'll get your shape back if you stop now.'

'No one wants tits at their belly button.'

In front of the oval mirror in the wardrobe, part of his parent's original bedroom suite, he'd made her look at herself naked. Using a pencil as a pointer to her enlarged brown nipples. And then putting the pencil under each breast where it stuck fast. Not rolling down her stomach like it used to so that he'd laugh and kiss her pale cone breasts. He tried to make her ashamed of her new full shape.

They'd fallen downwards and round in the second month of pregnancy, with dark veins a network of purple activity. They mapped her breasts with a new meaning. She bought maternity bras with white lace to hide them from him. Size 14B. They made her pointy and fortress-like and he stayed away.

When the baby was overdue — three days, a week, then two weeks and a day, he went out more at nights — coming home smelling of a pub toilet and very concerned that his little cyclist hadn't yet pedaled out. One night, it was nearly twelve, he said the baby must have broken a chain in there. The image was terrifying. She thought strangely of her miniature son trapped inside; his tiny toes gripped to the pedals of a toy bike; the pedals going round so madly but getting nowhere at all because the chain was missing. She held on tightly to the snoring elbow of the man beside her and whispered in the moon turning room for something to happen. Alone, alone, except for the pointed kicks inside when least she was expecting them.

It was Autumn and already cold when she went back to her old job. He never let her take the car though she was up well before five to have everything ready. She left two pieces of thick Tip Top in the toaster, water in the kettle, two spoons of tea in the pot and the butter out of the fridge so he couldn't say it was too hard to spread. She worked methodically and fast, neatly cutting his devon and tomato sauce sandwiches and stacking them in triangles of two into his blue tupperware lunchbox.

Her breasts were still heavy with milk. She ached to feel them warm and full inside her jumper. Instead of the tablets, she expressed milk. In the freezer there were always three or more bottles; ice cold and waiting for Alice the baby minder to thaw them out slowly on Lo. She underlined this instruction, hating to think of her baby drinking burnt milk through a rubber nipple.

The first time she expressed milk in front of him, was her first day back at work. She stayed in bed under the warm blankets wishing her baby wasn't such a good morning sleeper. With his sleep-smelly breath, he told her what an old cow she was:

'A bloody milkmaid.'

'A bloody martyr, milking herself like that.'

He'd grabbed a breast to make milk squirt; dug his finger tips under the flop and asked where was the girl he married. She smelt fish — prawns rotting under his nails from the night before.

Because it was dark and the mist thick outside, she wore a plastic scarf tied under her chin to keep her hair dry and a black raincoat. He yelled she needed a broom not a bike. Yelled from their bedroom window so she worried about the neighbours, that the little man would wake and howl, make her milk run. A fight at five thirty in the morning of her first day back. Then, she cried with hurt. But she is remembering these things now so her leave taking will be easy. No goodbyes. Like a cat in shadow she will disappear and not be found.

The bike she'd used for work was one of his clapped out racers. Italian wheels and all, but too heavy he said. 'A bit like you, ha ha.' His laugh was like gunshot. Before the baby, she'd once ripped a cheesecloth skirt, swinging her leg over the tall bike's bar. She remembers his laugh then as aroused and persistent, he pushed her against the cold tin wall and urged himself on. Working it out from her *Everywoman*, her mother's kitchen tea gift, she noted the date as Conception Day. Anzac Day, ironically enough.

As the bike chain was very loose, she wheeled the bike to work for something to lean on, to hold tight to. If the chain fell off it was impossible in the early morning dark to get it back on. With the mist and the black grease on cold metal, she would nearly cry. So on her first day back to work, even with his angry voice coming from the house, she'd wheeled the bike.

She'd named the green-rusting bike Buntie. She told Buntie about baby, his small fingers, his fat legs. She sang a lullaby, half asleep and her feet making their own way down the road. *Bye baby bunting, Daddy's gone a hunting*.

In the time she'd been away, a new blue container had been placed in the corner of every cubicle. The containers were of two toned blue plastic and replaced the tin buckets there before. Peeling instructions told cleaners not to empty the new device. Tampons and pads dissolved inside. Impossible to see into the narrow containers. The lids were designed to only show blue. She read the trade name. RENTAKILL. Rent and kill. Violent words.

There was a dampness climbing the walls of the public amenities and the disinfectant filled her nose. Being the end of school holidays, lots of traffic going north through the town, the toilets were a filthy mess. The old mop stank grey and ancient as the cement cubicle walls. Spare toilet rolls, toppled from a precarious shelf into puddles, sat like toads. She tried not to think of her sweet smelling baby, alone in his cot, waiting for Alice to change and feed him. On the tin roof, camphorlaurel berries fell as sadly as tears.

When almost all the Ladies was clean, her milk spurted through her shirt. She felt it warm and thin the moment she heard the crying. Someone was crying small and sad from the Mens next door.

Outside it was still dim; a milky dawn. She needed a torch and remembered at the last moment her bike lamp. It was kittens! She recognised their mewls before the light beam picked out the two black bodies crawling blindly in circles. 'Little kitty, kitty, kitty.'

They were tiny. Less than a few weeks old. She wrapped them in her jumper and put them into a hand basin so they'd keep each other quiet and warm. They were damp and shivering. She could feel the trembles inside them as her hand curled over their bodies. Too young to purr. Daylight through the gaps near the ceiling reminded her there were another six toilets to clean as well as the urinal. In her absence, she'd forgotten the penis graffiti of men's toilets; the crude pictures like clubs. 'This is the exact size of my dick,' beneath a drawing looped halfway across a wall. There was a smell of urine and shit. 'Here's my nine inch chic stick.' The words made her feel ill. She hated to think of picking up her baby after putting her hands near unclean toilets, scrubbing forever, it seemed, at the cold seats and stains that wouldn't go away.

Seeing the body half flushed down, wet and floating fur, the tail bent up against the dirty porcelain bowl — it was impossible not to retch. It would've been a pretty cat, she could tell, with white whiskers and feet. The head was jammed down inside the loop so she had to plunge her hands into the water and pull. Yellow rubber gloves filled with toilet water. 'Poor kitty. Poor kitty.' She cried, thinking of her old child self, who not very long ago always owned a cat. 'The little cat girl,' her Grandma Addy used to say to see her down at the cow bails, dishing out milk to the latest litter of thin kittens. When she married, her husband mentioned asthma, fleas, hair, allergies.

So she felt brave when she wheeled home the two stray kittens in the basket of her bike. For two days she managed to hide them. But looking in the laundry for some wood glue he'd misplaced, he found their box and trod in the kitty litter.

He laughed. He was in a good mood. Called her a cheeky thing and said she could keep one. Then took the smallest kitten away and knocked its head with a hammer on the cement footpath. Or twisted. She heard the scrunch; the thin bones. As it was garbage night, he put the kitten in the bin, freezer-bag-wrapped with a twist tie. She meant to bury the tiny body when he was sleeping but too late the clang of the morning garbos woke her.

A couple of years later, his promotion came through. He said it was time she gave up work to spend more time with his kid. The baby minder was costing as much as she earned.

She began to read her son stories. Cat ones were good, she told her son. 'Three little kittens had three little mittens,' 'The Owl and the Pussycat went to sea in a beautiful pea green boat,' 'The cat in the hat,' 'The cat who went to heaven,' which was an old favourite of hers. She borrowed them from the public library and loved to read to him.

When he reached kindergarten age, he learnt how to draw a cat. Two circles, stick whiskers, sharp ears and a circling tail. He painted his cat black with green eyes and gave it to her. She stuck it on the fridge and keeps it still.

So it's funny she thinks, that he ends up like his father, not liking the sleek, black cat that was a kitten when he was only a baby. She contemplates the past and present as she attacks the toilet of the house for which they've just paid a deposit. The house is weatherboard with the outside dunny down from the house. Years of old urine have caked into a thick brown shell and she's abandoned the spikey bog brush for a chisel. In the slow spinning sun on the grass, her cat basks and watches her: pats at the small lizards on the garden path, unsheaths and sheaths dark claws into the grass. From faraway, comes the sounds of her son on his tricycle — a big three wheeler with squeaking pedals. She hacks at the toilet bowl, gradually chipping away the mess to reveal a cleaner white below. She thinks, 'I will leave on Anzac Day!' And is suddenly delighted with the symmetry of things her husband will never recognise, or her son.

The tricycle sounds come closer. He's going flat out round the side of the house and yelling out. He has his father's angry eyes, the colour of acid blue milk. A large raspberry gobstopper distorts one cheek and has reddened his lips.

'Wanna go. Mummy. I wanna go to the toilet. Wanna go.' He's hurtling down the cement pathway, aims to run over the cat's tail and narrowly misses the white tip. She's heavy with kittens and sun and slower to spring out of his way.

'Mummy, Mummy. Wanna go!'

In the silent corners of the out house ceiling, she sees there is an army of small grey watch spiders. Their webs are shadow grey and quiet.

She cries, 'careful,' as he tips the bike over and makes for the toilet. He's wearing a miniature sized racing singlet with the motif of his father's cycling club on it: two wheels interlocked and dizzying in an optical illusion of movement.

'Wait for me,' she orders. He flashes a disarming grin, pulls down his shorts and stands facing the toilet like a grown man. He pees all over the place, splashes it on his feet. He aims higher. At the spiders. At the shiny sky through the holes in the roof.

'Look Mummy!' He smiles at the yellow patterns he's making but she's turning away. She stands outside and picks up her cat, carefully because of the babies inside. A daylight moon hangs straight above them. He's yelping for her attention but she's seeing the face of his father after the pain was over in the labour ward he'd stayed away from: hearing his voice ask if it took long for a baby's eyes to open. As if a baby was a pup, a kitten.

Her son's piddle is losing height. She hears his voice go all desperate and high and turns toward him. He's swinging his small penis in determined circles, shrieking, 'Look Mummy, look. I'm looping the loop.'

Board Games

Damien is animated, describing to Linda all the times his life has nearly been stuffed up by other people. He works backwards from adolescence to when he was very young. She lies stretched in the plastic curve of the sun chair, staring at the pool water and the dying lawn beyond. This summer is too burnt for real grass. Around the pool's edge there's a thin border of turquoise plastic. A child skids over its tricking surface. In the blood and skin of the grazed knees, plastic grass slivers, cling and shine green-blue.

The howls of the child disturb Damien's smooth story. Linda can see how he's suddenly on edge. Abruptly he leaves his chair and dives into the water. The splashes reaching her legs are tepid. The pool isn't deep, four foot at most and by mid morning it's like swimming in dirty bath water. Where she works every other day except Wednesdays, the pool is identical. Heart shaped, lukewarm and kids piling up like sunburnt cupids in the bubbling spa when she's working a day shift. If only yesterday's pollution hadn't been so obvious and bouyant while she was waiting for a wave, she'd be at the beach now. But such visibility was too much. She'd left the water immediately; pushing her way through the thick undertow and the crowd of swimmers in their ragged formations between the flags.

Linda hasn't told him she works. Damien hasn't asked and seems to assume she's on holiday, single and just as fascinated by his perverse childhood as he has always been himself. She watches his shoulders ploughing up the water. He's doing freestyle like an athlete until he hits his head on the concrete side of the far curve. She wishes he'd sink.

As he hauls his dripping body from the water, she untangles her sunglasses from her hair and puts them back on. They're deep black and deceptive so he can believe she's watching his progress back to her with admiration. It's a game she can't stop playing. Really, she has shut her eyes unable to bear, even through expensively tinted, prescription glass, that green bulging nylon between his legs.

'Linda, can I get you a drink?' He stands so close there's water dripping on her stomach. 'You should go in for a dip,' he shakes his head so the water spins from his hair all over her. Linda lifts her glasses. A girl in a string bikini walks past with a bright, tall cocktail.

'I'll have one of those thanks.'

'Pardon,' Damien says.

'I'll have a cocktail like that girl has.'

'Right,' he fishes enthusiastically in the folds of his towel, which is a lighter shade of green to match his little speedos. There's a one hundred dollar note sitting inside his soft cotton bag and, almost with a flourish, he extracts it. The note is like monopoly money, thin and blue looking. Linda wonders if he really thinks a few frosted cocktails and stories of a strange mother can buy her.

Thoroughly, precisely, he rubs himself down. All over, the towel is whisked: across his curiously hairless arms, in between those hairier legs. For a moment it seems he executes a frontal pose. Smiling with his gums, he stands with his legs confident and apart so she must see the dark, long shadow under his wet swimmers. That decides her. She'll piss him off before lunch. She hates men who think they're a Cleo centrefold.

Damien waves from the queue at the tropical bark-hut bar — not an open palmed wave but trying to be cute, using only his fingers. His whole posture is attempting masculinity but there's something effeminate about his body. Or is it only his thin bird hair, crested and peaked in waves?

132

Their Blue Hawaii's are so lurid they have to squint to drink them. Hanging at jaunty angles from the glasses are miniature paper umbrellas and chopped pineapple. Damien sucks his swizzle stick seductively, his thick red tongue curling backwards and forwards around pink plastic breasts.

Linda notices his bullet head, flat and blunt behind the hair he keeps fluffing to hide its recession. And also that his teeth have yellow stains running down from his gums. The sort of teeth that could indicate some terrible and deprived childhood. He is still telling her about it.

'I don't think it's affected me as badly as it could of.'

Could have. Could Have. Linda internally corrects. For a year she taught grammatical English and her response is automatic.

'Being dressed as a girl until I was seven. I can remember my hair. There's photos you know, of me with blonde, curling tresses,' he sucks his straw hard and gurgles air at the bottom of his glass. 'My mother used to coil it all up into tight stockings. Every night and wet my head to make it set. She'd turn me into a doll for school every morning and my sister into my brother. Role reversals, you know. I was Rosalind and my sister was Damien. Wacky. I was like a princess. There's a whole photo album. It was school that found out I wasn't. 'When I wouldn't pee after chocolate milk at recess, a teacher marched me into a cubicle and saw.'

Linda crunches her pineapple and combs creamy pink conditioner through her hair. The strong musk smell interrupts his narrative flow. He fiddles at his body with his legs thrown open, ruffling the hairs that gather so densely on his inner thighs. He says his childhood fucked him up but he doesn't talk about it that way. Rather, as if it's made him quite exceptional — more desirable than other men. 'I've still got a feminine sensitivity. I know how Chinese women with bound feet were. Restricted. Powerless. That was me until I was seven years old.' He's full of amazement. Perhaps

133

it's a new revelation. 'My anima's really strong.'

Linda's almost asleep and pings open a chinese cotton fold up sun hat. It's white with colourful paint thumb prints. She tries to read meanings into the diminishing circles that compose each thumb. She notices none of the thumbprints are identical. Lots of thumbs must have been used in the decoration of her hat. It's not that Linda's disinterested in Damien's stories but the sun and bacardi and all her late shifts have made her tired.

Damien looks at his swatch. It's an expensive design with flags. 'Nearly midday,' he says, 'How about some lunch?'

Linda sees her stomach is blotching red-purple and feels the itchiness of sunburn beginning. She's never liked sunbaking but where she works they expect deep brown skin so that teeth look white, eyeballs, but especially breasts under dim lights when she bends over to serve some old bastard a double scotch or a frothing cocktail special. Her uniform is small with a loose V-neck designed to plunge open and excite the customers just a little bit when she takes orders and serves them drinks. The first night she wore a bra and was reprimanded. 'Got to be a bit nice, eh?' and had to slip it off.

Damien is waiting for her answer. 'No thanks,' says Linda. 'I never eat lunch,' and is angry at herself for feeling guilty. His face has crumpled. He thinks she has rejected him and his uniquely horrible upbringing. Her pity alarms her. She's been married and since leaving, hasn't established any close relationships with men. Looking at Damien's crestfallen body, even his legs are shut together, she thinks there is something in all men that makes her respond the way she did towards her ex. With Damien it's her terrible rush of pity, a temptation to relent.

Linda left her marriage the morning of a dying party where a few hours before, her husband of eighteen months had begged the band that if they kept playing, they could all fuck his wife. He let them. She let them. Everyone, but most of all her husband, wanted the music to keep going. In the despair of the seedy new day, because of it, she rolled her husband off her body and left. He clutched out at one breast, sang the infuriating jingle for the electric blanket, brand-named 'Linda', then went back to sleep, his mouth wet and open. Not a difficult leavetaking.

Easier still to abandon Damien to his holiday. Return to square one, Dame. Linda is smug, not sad anymore. Ignoring his dejection, she slips on a big shirt, her sandals, her hat, glasses, bag over shoulder, and says she has to be going. She ruffles his hair like he's a kid and says something deliberately corny like, 'keep travelling north pal.'

The sound of cars from the highway, the exhaust and haze, seem worse in the midday heat. And the pale strip of ocean is as milky as the dregs in the row of cocktail glasses between their two empty chairs. Damien watches her walk off but she doesn't look over her shoulder.

Back at her flat, Linda takes out a big tub of mixed gelato. The colours have melted into each other and don't look inviting and fresh anymore. She tastes a fraction of lemon on a teaspoon. Really though, she told Damien the truth. She's not hungry and she hardly ever eats lunch. Also, the glass jar of olives going mouldy inside her fridge door has reminded her of one of Damien's middle teenage chapters. For five days his mother kept him locked in her pantry. To survive, he ate preserved fruit and vegetables in elaborate, decorative shapes; his mother's best mango chutney. There was hardly any smell because of good ventilation and the airtight efficiency of tall pickle bottles. He told the episode in great detail, as a rivetting story of oppression. Only he ruined the suspense by confessing, halfway through, of his vast enjoyment of the district exhibits at the Easter Show. All those rows and patterns of pickle jars he has such a fondness for, the domesticity of the bottled choko, cut into stars. Just the style favoured by his mother!

Linda congratulates herself on a lucky escape. Anyone speaking so reverentially of pickled choko would have to have been a pervert in bed. She wonders if perhaps all people's lives aren't awful. Not an original thought she knows but it's the kind of thinking she likes to jot down in her diary. She pulls out a big blue Collins notebook, one of many she stole before leaving the Department of Education, and impressively writes, 'perhaps all people's lives are awful. A dreadful proposition but true I think.' Before she can spot the pomposity and scribble it out, she snaps shut the diary and jams it back under the kapocky mattress.

Linda's own parents were always old and odd to her. In fact her father is ten years younger than her mother but both have old fashioned names: Sidney and Majella. Linda was a mistake that happened when Majella was forty. Linda has always thought it miraculous she wasn't born with a pointy head or water on the brain.

Usually she tries to hide her feet.' Your only defect darling,' her private school prickhead of a husband enjoyed pointing out. 'They betray your working class antecedents.' Because her middle toes were at least a centimetre longer than her big toe.

Linda flops onto her bed, covered in the bright white chenille Majella bought her when they came through on their holiday. A fan revolves above her bed too slowly to relieve the heat. The fan is wood with brass blades so shiny she can see her reflection. She switches on the radio of her digital clock. The volume has to be up very loud or else all she hears is noisy static. Absently, she fingers the spikiness of her legs, they need a shave, and her prickling bikini line. In the curving blades she sees her body small and anxious and only a bit distorted. She's reminded of something, somebody.

The aluminium windows of the flat frame a couple of orange, hopeless hibiscuses, wilting in the heat. She watches the flowers while her fingers open her body and tickle. She's white and brown: the colours of a split macadamia. Her skin smells of chlorine, guanine and some sweeter scent still. It's an oddly repelling mixture, too much summer, and she increases the pace of her finger and fantasy so she can be finished and have a shower.

A song on the radio stops her; the old Wings song about Uncle Albert; sadder and more plaintive because she has an Uncle Albert, if only just. He's dying in her old bedroom at her parent's flat in Allawah, Sydney. The Christmas Uncle, she used to call him as a small girl, because he usually had Christmas dinner with them and never failed to give Linda a good present.

The morning Linda left her husband, she took a bus, then a train from the Eastern Suburbs to home. Not home really because her parents only moved there in her last year at Teachers College and three months later she'd moved out and was married. The line south was almost empty it was so early and everyone travelling in the other direction. She thought she'd stay for a few days, totally forgetting Uncle Albert had been moved into her old bedroom. 'For good,' her parents whispered. 'He's going downhill real quick.' They tip toed into the bedroom, it wasn't even seven o'clock. Her mother was wrapped tightly in the pink and nylon quilting of a dressing gown and old Sid just stood there looking down. Enough to ring Linda's heart. She remembers that sentimental and dramatic entry to her diary: 'My heart is wrung!' No one had ever bothered to take down the tizzy chantilly curtains, most of her posters were still there and the white laminex built ins and dressing table with red plastic knobs. Only the bed was in a different position. Uncle Albert wasn't sleeping secure, tucked round himself, but sprawled out, flung as though from a horse in a violent fall. He had shrunk into an ancient child, sucking his thumb. Sid and Maj, even though they carried more weight, were shrinking too Linda noticed when she hugged them. For her, it was strange to know how two brothers brought up on a dairy farm, all that free calcium, could succumb to osteoporosis and just shrivel away.

Linda showers, washes her hair, shaves under her arms and scratches a pimple between her breasts. Her husband had a lot of small red pimples on his backside and a fleshy face.

As Linda steps out of the shower, there's a smell of lime air freshener seeping through her carpet. The cleaner is in the stairwell, dispersing imaginary bad smells with her aerosal can. From her window Linda sees the line of dark bunya pines, telegraph wires, the beer garden on the corner, kids in swimmers with icecreams running on zebra crossings toward the beach. She wishes she hadn't talked to Damien. His immersion in memory has initiated a cold plunge into her own. She gets out a new pair of Olympus binoculars and focuses them on the beach: all that glistening skin. She can almost smell the bodies frying up in coconut oil. Suddenly she spies, *I spy with my little eye, something beginning with D:* Damien in grey and red and even tinier speedos, chatting up a topless girl with plaits. Linda laughs and wonders about that embroidered cotton shoulder bag he carries. Does it contain a multitude of lycra flashing swimwear? And do his stories change with the colours? She unfocuses the lenses until he's just a bright blur, then progresses along the beach. Under a red and white striped umbrella a fat lady sleeps. Linda watches her burning breasts rising and falling. There are three fat toddlers with buckets and spades. They're building castles; humpty ones with internal tunnels and moats for the tide to fill when it rises. Their excitement seems so close as each wave washes a little nearer. Linda tilts the binoculars up a fraction and then all there is, is the sea gliding by, blue blurred and white.

It's after two and Linda makes herself a herbal tea. Sitting watching the peppermint swirl in patterns to the bottom of the cup she tries to remember her own childhood sea days. Hard to pin down how many big family holidays there were with uncles and lots of aunts, sprawled across a headland in small caravans and tents for the children. Best, she remembers the one with Uncle Albert, or maybe there were lots of holidays with him, but she only remembers the one where there was the big sand castle on the beach every morning. Each morning she'd follow Uncle Albert along the sand and just before the rockpools there'd always be the gigantic sandcastle with turrets. And stones and shells pressed in patterns into the walls. The castle was almost as tall as herself and always in the same position where the incoming tide would destroy it. So really it wouldn't have mattered if she did scramble over, as she longed to do, kicking it down and making the sand fly. But she never dared. Uncle Albert would be walking away with his fishing rod and she'd stand in front of the castle, indecisive and awed at the size: so more mysterious because she'd never seen the builder. The castle appeared in the night it seemed, to be waiting there for her in the early morning when the sea was green and see through. In the end she'd always run to catch her uncle. She never took the decision to destroy the castle quickly. By the time they came back it would be half eroded into curving foundations, the stones and shells sunk into wet, ordinary sand.

Linda is repainting her mouth and eyes. Life is ordinary and repetitious after childhood, a boardgame that won't finish or thrill anymore. She uses red lipstick and carefully turns her mouth into a tiny, erotic and sad hole. Her lips tell her she could never have been innocent.

Suddenly her eyes are caught by a pink circle on her

bedspread. It smells of musk and hair oil and makes her angry. She hates to forget things like conditioner through her hair. The thought of starting work at six, all those leering men through to the early hours, becomes so unbearable, she decides to quit. She'd intended sticking it out for another month at least but couldn't be bothered now. These days, she's more impulsive about journeys.

Dave, the manager of the Sunshine Playbox, begins to abuse her over the phone. She hangs up, unable to care they'll be short staffed. Quitting with no notice means no pay for the three nights she has worked this week already but she feels immediately happier.

Her old history tutor and lover is a free spirit and always glad to see her. He runs the best Vegetarian Mexican restaurant on the North Coast. She just feels like some decent food and an uncrowded beach.

Starting with her bedspread, Linda begins to pack. She's not methodical and leaves behind her diary, three cheese shaped fridge magnets with Sydney postcards underneath, two bottles of expensive hair bath on top of the shower, melting gelato in the kitchen and all consideration of her five hundred dollar bond.

Only after racing her last traffic light and well away on the black speeding highway does the question of bond money occur to her. She'll ring tomorrow and try to get it back through the post. He's an understanding sort her real estate agent. Since she has slept with him once it shouldn't be too difficult. She's driving fast with one hand balanced on the gear stick. Absentmindedly, she removes all trace of the sunset rose lipstick with her tongue.

It Gets Late Early

The biro wouldn't work. A new black bic but no amount of scribbling, dotting or vigorous rubbing between both hands seemed to be doing any good. Remembering a school kid habit Sid used to get ropable over, Majella used her teeth to pull off the plastic pen cap. Then she took out the skinny, ink filled tube and sucked hard. The ink filled her mouth suddenly. She spat into a pink Kleenex. The colour was old, clotted blood and Majella bent closer to her table, hoping no one had seen. With a burst of inspiration she put two disprin on her tongue. They fizzed away at the ink, ticklish, making her giggle.

This time, the pen worked immediately, blobbing across the shiny paper. Now Majella could fret properly over her first cruise post card. She imagined the pen grew heavy in her fingers, poised expectantly above the comma following Dear Linda. From the silver glomesh bag fanned a dozen or more postcards, all with the same picture; yet to be written. Majella sighed, tasted ink at the back of her throat and wondered whether it might be best to leave her daughter to lucky last. The sound of the rain was lulling with the piped music. Easy to doze. Fighting off such an easy escape from holiday duties, Majella bought herself a coffee with scones. The clotted cream and strawberry conserve took away the taste of leaked Bic ink. Afterwards, she felt fortified enough to begin her daughter's postcard with a description of their boat's wonderful meals.

A guilty conscience made her add that the big spring swells were making Sid sick. Only after it was written, did Majella realize how bad that sounded coming right after bacon and eggs with grilled tomatoes. She scratched at the eczema breaking up in patches on her left cheek. Majella had a feeling the airconditioning was affecting her skin. The salt air maybe. No amount of Oil of Ulan could stem the tide of flaking skin, despite her vigilance: the morning, night and midday drenchings in the pink moisturiser that promised so much.

Eventually, Majella signed off with a flourish, very satisfied after all. With the obligatory weather details recorded, the card looked crammed with news. She prided herself on a thorough approach to postcards. Especially with Linda, who stuck all such correspondence under fridge magnets, where any odd bod could pick them off and read.

Once the address had been squeezed in, the stamp only just fitted. Everything was how it should be. A cruise attendant fluttered up to her and past, whisking away the jam Majella was about to polish off with her teaspoon. Not even this loss could detract from Majella's cosy feelings. With Linda's prototype card before her, she began to fill in other cards, all fourteen of them, sustained by a few more rounds of scones. She replaced the offending bit about Sidney with: 'Sid crook first few days. On road to recovery now. Pleased to say!'

But Sidney wasn't on the road to anywhere. Today was the fourth he'd refused to get up for. He moped, feeling queasy and full of hate for the picture of triangular yachts on the wall. Each day he spent a good few hours perched on the toot, reading the ship's paper, missing the form guide of the Daily Telly and watching television. The toilet seat was the only place to sit where he didn't get a cricked neck but no racing had been televised so far and at any rate there was no real way of having a bet. Today was apparently to be Japanese baseball again. It annoyed the life out of Majella to find him sitting there, so he kept doing it though secretly her dire premonitions about bottom germs were getting to him. Albert's germ had been the end of him. Just a little germ by all accounts, but the last straw. To combat these growing worries, Sidney covered the seat with reams of folded toilet paper. Yank, yank, yank. In the middle of the night if he just had to go, he could sense Majella's agitation as he ripped away at the paper. She said the embarrasment was keeping her awake, particularly after the incident with their cabin attendant.

'Could you do us a favour and fetch us a few more date rolls?'

'Sir?'

'Afraid we're almost out of date roll.'

'With your breakfast tray?'

'Don't be a dope. Dunny Paper!'

Sidney chuckled into his fat chin thinking of his wife's indignation. He flicked through the ship's daily newspaper. Not up to scratch, he'd noticed several spelling botches, though he appreciated the attempt at a page three girl. The story flanking the tall blonde model was about the fining of a barmaid for indecent behaviour. She'd removed the see-through top in order to dip her breasts into drinkers' beer. Bloody disgusting, Sidney thought and wondered whether the girl's name was familiar because he'd once taught her. He often read things in the local paper at home about the misdemeanours of former students. In his retirement year, two sixth form girls were raped on their way home from the end of the year party. It made him wonder — how women led men on and then changed their minds afterwards.

A sudden nosebleed splatted across the newsprint but Sidney stayed calm. Nosebleeds happened fairly regularly these days. He let his face sink into a wad of rose coloured toilet paper and waited for the blood, so salty now in his throat, to subside.

In another cabin, Sunshine Pine Economy and therefore two levels closer to the hull than Sidney and Majella's

143

room, Teddie Arthurs lay seasick, half in, half out of his hot bed. One hand held an American Penthouse limply aloft, while the other moved feebly on his unstiffening penis. In just four days he'd discovered that during orgasm was the only time his queasy feelings abated. But he'd read the forum letters so often now and peeled back the little black ovals from the womens' pubic hair, that he could hardly be excited anymore. His erection subsided completely as a tune from South Pacific, *A hundred and one, Piles of fun*, was interrupted by a reminder that afternoon activities were to be held under shelter on Aloha Deck. Gloomily, Teddie wondered whether anyone would bother to be his partner in the coconut cracking competition. The memories of being the outcast of school birthday parties: that terrible pass the orange game, no hands but chin to chin, boy to girl, so you could pretend to be necking, haunted him still. An exclusion that couldn't be forgotten after only a couple of years on the clerical staff of the Audits section for the local council.

Teddie yanked at his dank sheets and watched the clock imitating the frustrating patterns of his life and holiday. Beneath the sheet, his groin felt drained and aching with that dull emptiness. He calculated the coconut game would have started. Too late already to change his mind. He walked across to the mirror that made him dizzy, suspended as it was on a long notch of photographed timber wall paper. Overnight, a row of pimples had marched in a curve from Teddie's left ear down his neck. Worse still, he could sense more irritation, an entirely new battalion, marshalling behind his other ear lobe. He felt disgusting, poxy, pussy but allowed his fingernails to begin the squeeze job ahead. Each fleck of white was wiped on the wallpaper around the mirror. By the end of the three weeks, he thought, the army assaulting his neck would have transferred into an armada of yellow dots, circumnavigating the glass. Like a sea explorer down to using his own blood for ink, he could mark his boredom in pus, write letters in it. *Hi fellas. Gidday Meric. Thought I'd send a pus postcard to let you know how I'm getting along.*

The pulse of Teddie's neck was so slow and strong it ended up interfering with the popping. He abandoned his systematic fingernails for a more potent remedy. From out of his blue plastic toilet bag, emblazoned in red writing that listed the countries of the world, he removed his mother's solution. The familiar mix, metho, tea-tree and eucalyptus oil and other less identifiable ingredients, conjured up odours of his confused and dogged childhood. Headlice, haematomas, tickbites, bruises — Teddie's Mum believed she could tackle anything. The mixture stung like crazy; felt like a hundred bush ants were biting his face. Then the fumes swam into his face, worse than onions or shampoo, and he could cry at last.

At lunchtime, Majella returned to her cabin with sandwiches for Sid, a cup of tea and a slice of cheesecake. Sidney was asleep though, making the noises of a milk heavy cow. She sighed. The room was even beginning to smell sour. She placed the food tray next to his teeth which floated gently, moving in a special, constricted rhythm of their own. Somehow, it all seemed too reminiscent of the last weeks with Albert: the smell of cheese which was all Albert would eat despite the constipating effects: the painful snore.

Majella hurried to find one of her large print romances, out on special extended loan from her municipal library. The setting was a cruise, with similar port destinations as Majella's own. She looked forward to immersing herself. Much as Sidney wasn't enjoying things, she felt full of expectations of pleasure. This was her cruise — not any old holiday up the coast. The dull old North Coast that was going ahead so slowly, littered with the grey cow bails leaning for the earth. Majella wished to see the rusting sheds fall over forever. She liked the towns that were wiping out the sour smelling past with hardiplank, brick veneer and colourbond fencing. Linda was different. For her final year art project at school she'd submitted a series of photographs titled 'Moreton Bay Memory.' Majella remembered the praise of Linda's art teacher but couldn't see anything special herself in a lot of old moreton bay figtrees towering over dirty rotten tin sheds. Or the disturbing close ups of ancient root systems: Majella thought they looked like entwined limbs of old people and told Linda she couldn't hang them on the walls.

Beryl Ruby Rabbit always stayed in a caravan park on the North Coast for her holidays. This thought made Majella feel superior and rather glamorous. She was at sea, aboard a luxury liner. Sidney was not feeling the best, that was true, but Majella comforted herself with the knowledge that had they been on one of their normal holidays, Sidney would only be in a pub.

Today, Majella was anxious to spot a real romance in the developing stages, in order that she could follow its progress during the cruise, through to a soft, passionate end.

How disappointing then, that the young funeral director of last night's acquaintance should again pull a chair towards her. He grinned. Majella's shoulders huddled involuntarily. He offered her some salad. All that was left were a few oily bits of cucumber he seemed to have avoided. Even though it would give her the burps, Majella politely chased a slice around the garlickey bowl.

'Where's Sidney then Majella?'

'Not feeling the best,' she said, letting the cucumber seeds slide down. 'Really a pity.'

'No sea legs yet?'

'No,' Majella wished he'd leave. Not healthy for such a young man to be so intimately involved in death. Or so friendly and talkative to old people like herself. Last night he'd been saying how as a young kid he used to play hide and seek in the empty coffins. More significantly, his presence prompted anxious thoughts, making her think again of the recent death of Albert in the spare room. The young funeral director proffering further polite cucumber, leant closer in an unpleasant way.

Albert hadn't taken long to die. Like any of his other visits over the years, he'd been a good guest. A bit of a wag, not a big eater and always good for tips.

'She's getting wusser all the time,' Albert liked to joke about Beryl upstairs who came to see him every Friday afternoon.

'It gets late early,' he whispered in winter. His last winter.

Majella mused. Morbid. Wondering what scraps people would recall about herself. Something like, 'She loved a baked leg of lamb on Sundays.' Majella could hear Beryl Ruby Rabbit saying that.

'The rain looks spectacular over the sea,' said the funeral director. His name, she remembered suddenly, was William.

'Yes,' Majella fished gingerly for prawns in the avocado he'd insisted she try. 'Makes it nice to be indoors'.

'Dad often wanted to paint the sea.'

'Mmmm?'

'Yes!' he scooped avocado energetically and sprayed her with green spit. 'Or a sea burial. Something ignored by artists these days.' He was on the verge of telling her about the paint by numbers masterpiece he bought in toyshops on this very subject matter. They were all sunsets, melodramatic skies and people, nothing cutprice or budget about them. Quality, William labelled them — Made in Great Britain. However, Majella began to speak first.

'Bit gloomy for a painting isn't it?' she said. 'I've always preferred something bright. Fruit in a bowl. Or horses. You'd have to go a long way to find something better than horses for a painting.'

To make Albert's dying easier, Majella had bought a

147

silver stallion landscape for him to watch. Sidney propped form guides in front of his brother's nose so that the white sheets turned grey.

William ahemed so hard his lips trembled. Majella already had them sized up as weak lips, and his teeth were too brown and pointy to ever kiss a young woman seductively.

'Do you like to play cards,' he began. 'With the rain I thought maybe five hundred, whist . . .'

'Bugger,' Majella groaned with irritation. The bandaid on her finger had come unstuck with the agitation of her fingers. Underneath was the neat slice from the potato peeler. It leaked watery blood. She had to put the cut to her mouth to suck, tasting salt and little warm bits of disintegrating skin. It was as good an excuse as any to withdraw from her unwelcome companion. She did so immediately, into the safety of the women's rest rooms.

William, the young but confident funeral director felt his weak stomach turn at the sight of the discarded bandaid. Muddy composites did not agree with him: blood against green avocado. He decided to return to his cabin and see what Teddie was up to.

'Are you having a good time?' Teddie was over eager with a girl he thought looked as left out as himself. Within seconds of spotting her solitary position, he'd created a birthday party past as miserable and lonely as his own.

'Yes,' said the girl, without sounding convinced. 'I'm watching the horizon.'

Teddie waited, hopeful of some other revelation, more personal, but she wasn't looking at him.

'By the way I'm Ted. Or Teddie if you want.'

She nodded but didn't name herself. So Teddie kept wandering, up to a higher deck where there was no one in sight. A couple of middle aged women surprised him from their position in a sheltered corner. They wore fluffy cardigans round their shoulders but Teddie found he was still able to see their low slung breasts. Just below the floral line of their sarongs were goosebumps. He moved past the women quickly. They too were staring out to sea, or maybe at the sky, hoping for a burst of sun to feed their white skins. After lunch it seemed the afternoons grew dark. There'd been no spectacular moons, suns or stars. No romance.

The rain began again. Soaking. Salty. Teddie tasted it with his tongue and decided not to care that the water was already past the plastic of his jacket. He stomped along where passengers weren't meant to be, heading for the outermost rail. Rain always made him want to go. He blamed this on his mother's paranoia on wet days at Infants School, when she dressed them all in flannel undies to keep the kidneys warm.

Teddie peed out over the side, leeward so the wind didn't blow it back in his face. He felt a certain satisfaction, wondering if any of his fellow passengers, any of the seven hundred so intent upon ignoring him, would see the rain turn briefly, palely yellow. His new gold and blue thongs were hurting. But if he went back to his cabin William might be there and he was trying to avoid William. For Teddie couldn't help being embarrassed by the fact that he was on holiday with the town's youngest funeral director. That they'd been mates since third class didn't alter his feelings. Worse still, Meric reckoned they'd turn into poofters going away for three weeks together. So Teddie kept walking, up another deck, down the other side, down a deck and around. William said how great it was to have inherited his father's line of trade at such a young age. He made his father's death sound like a business asset. Apparently prospective customers were flocking his way. Will explained this initial flush of sucess in terms of him being lucky enough to start up on his own the year of a new variation to The Funeral Fund Act. This meant people could prearrange their funerals. 'You can save your dear ones hours of confusion and sadness by investing now,' ran the advertising in the local paper. A chart William had drawn up both repelled and fascinated Teddie: a death statistics graph, predicting that the town was about to peak in terms of older residents popping off. For Teddie, it was all a bit much, specially if he thought too hard about it. No sooner had a batch of dear old husbands been buried, than Will had all the widows cooking him casseroles or darning his socks.

Teddie was sopped through. He sweated inside the plastic jacket and could almost feel himself steaming up. A massage would be the thing. According to the ship brochures, everyone could have them. If only the flaming pimples between his shoulder blades would subside.

All his holiday expectations were caving in. Everything was unreal: as impossible and hazy as the couples who were thin, moving lines through the glass windows. So he felt cheered to see the horizon-watching-girl was still there, as bored and lonely as himself. As worried? He hoped hard and edged toward her on a sneaky diagonal.

'Hi,' he was trying for something casual but the word popped out too fast.

'Yes?' She kept looking beyond Teddie.

'Want to hear a joke,' without meaning to he'd plunged himself into a commitment to be funny.

'I'm feeling sick,' she groaned.

'Yeah, it's a good joke,' his mind was a maze of lost punchlines and beginnings; baby jokes muddling with chicken-crossing-the-road ones.

'That's why I'm watching the horizon. Dad used to say in the car, "look straight ahead!", to stop us all being sick.'

'It's called If You're Not Feeling Happy.' Perhaps the idea for this joke had blown in with the increasing wind.

'I think I'll vomit if I look anywhere else.'

'Well there was a sparrow you see, and he decided to

fly north instead of south during winter. Because he was a sort of different sparrow from all the rest, see. But he flew into the snow which made his wings ice over. And the next thing clunk, he hits the ground. Just when he thought he was totally stuffed and the cold would get him, a cow shitted right on top. Made the sparrow that warm he began to sing. Right at the top of his voice. Which was a mistake cause the farm cat came round the corner and ate him for brekky.'

Teddie halted abruptly, unable to muster together the three punchlines ending the joke.

'Gee, that's funny,' her sarcasm stung like the salt in his eyes but Teddie pretended not to notice. He stared out to the windy drizzle, looking for a horizon. In his mind, the Jumbo Book of Office Humour was sitting on Craigo the teaboy's small wood desk. That's where he dumped it on his last Friday afternoon before The Holiday. His Holiday. After completing the request to photocopy the sparrow joke and the one about a dog named Sex fifty three times for distribution to other council workers, Teddie thought he would have had them off by heart.

He sneaked a look at the seasick girl's face, hating her. 'Your face is green,' he said, suddenly triumphant because one of the punchlines at least had come back. About being warm and happy in a pile of shit and just staying put.

Teddie thought then that he should have stayed at home for his holidays and left the money in his 13% building society account. More than likely he would have had a better time with Cheryl who worked at Tickle's Pharmacy. Her breasts were warm and the free sample lipstick sweet, if he bought her enough bacardi and cokes on Friday nights.

That the funeral director lived in Albert's old town and therefore Sid's from childhood, made Majella vaguely alarmed. Thankgoodness he'd disappeared with the scraps from lunch. Yet Majella found she couldn't concentrate on her book. She tried to read, *Marielle looked shyly at his strong face, the red curling lips* . . . but could only think of death and greasy endings. She'd insisted Albert couldn't be burnt in his favourite old green jumper and provided one of Sid's. The night before the service, she'd put the evening's vegetable peelings into the rotten old jumper. She'd let her thin tears plop. She wrapped them up with muddy potato peel and threw everything away into the garbage. When Majella didn't cry at the crematorium, she could feel Sidney resented her, along with the plastic wrapped flowers. The small brass plate covering the opening where the ashes went, in a wallful of dead people, upset him most of all.

Majella hadn't minded that particular aspect so much. She thought the brass looked rather effective. That was until she heard on a radio talkback that live relatives weren't allowed to polish the plates. Everything was arranged to tarnish in certain patterns. The process and design was all worked out scientifically, the announcer explained to a distraught wife who'd been banned from using a rag and brasso on her dead husband's memorial plaque.

There was blood under the pillow case. During Sidney's afternoon sleep, the pillow slip had half wriggled off. When he opened his eyes the rusty blotch looked back. He felt panicky. People choked on nosebleeds in their sleep. A number one killer. But it was someone else's old blood. After waking up a bit and looking in the mirror, he realised his mistake. In the end though, he decided it was worse not belonging to him because now his mind was free to run through all the diabolic bleedings that may have taken place on his pillow. Unhygenic, unpleasant, he thought, and for the money he'd shelled out he expected more. Much more. He began to climb out of his pyjamas and into a shirt and jumper, staring with increasing irritation at the view from their cabin obscured by safety equipment. The cabin closed in on itself, poorly lit. As the daylight faded it meant switching on the lamp with the blink no one could fix.

Time to get up, queasy or not. On fluidy ankles he went to the wardrobe where Majella hung his clothes on the right hand side, the same as at home. He zipped himself up, forgetting underpants, so that later in the night, Majella would be bitterly embarrassed, having to introduce her husband as the man whose fly was undone, no jocks on underneath.

'C, for three points, O for one. That's three. W, that's four, seven and S makes eight!' William's obvious pleasure with the first word he'd used to begin the game, annoyed the life out of Teddie. So that regardless of Majella who completed the scrabble trio, he used the letter C to build crap instead of carp, for eight points also. As it was the Macquarie Australian Dictionary they were using to verify words, Teddie's contribution was allowed to stay on the board. Majella, however, hadn't taken part in the argument. She was staring at the letters and thinking anxiously of Sidney. About his health and his lack of holiday spirits. From the moment they'd walked up the boarding ramp, he'd dug his toes in like a poddy calf that wouldn't cross a bridge. And even though he'd been up and about tonight for dinner, he still wasn't right. Feeling defeated, she put down a word without much thought. Sadly for a first score of eleven. Teddie had drawn up a page of three columns but at this stage thought it less than likely the game could progress very far. Already they were hemmed into an awkward, deflated shape.

```
  C  O  W  S
  R
S A  D  L  Y
  P
```

Cows crap sadly. Majella thought of smelly green tails.

So did Teddie, thankful he was with the council and not with his father and brothers on the farm.

Will was eating musk sticks as well as lime chews and wondered about a connection between accelerating cancer fatalities and the chemicals consumed during childhood: the ones that made black jellybeans, orange battleships or green frogs, taste so good.

At the games table on their right, two little kids who'd been allowed to stay up, were joining the dots in a bored way. One boy was writing rude words on the pages of a magazine. Bum, poo, crap, bastard, dick. His sister swiped the black texta he was using. A tooth and fingernail fight began, hairpulling and strangling. They crashed against the scrabble game. Yellow letter squares flew into the air. The brother was on top so the girl's dress rucked up. Then she jabbed him in the balls. They both started to cry. Parents appeared. Sidney came round the corner with a beer and the children began to laugh and laugh at the sight of his wide open fly, the small wrinkled parts poking out: the pink, the purple.

Old Age Fairies

Eric Gilson reads his daughter's composition to his friends. He leaves it on his desk next to her photo. If he finds work impossible and too many cups of Andronicus, finely ground and plunged, are making his heart thump too fast, he picks up her story to read. The effect is always soothing.

Since Eric's heart seems to thump much more now he's separated from Janice and living on the border of the Sunshine State, he ends up knowing Jessica's story off by heart. Except for some Will Ogilvie verse he learnt at school and has never forgotten, Jessica's composition is the only bit of writing he likes to remember word for word. He can recite it with feeling in the cramped kitchen where the resonance is suprisingly good, or under a hot shower. Even the annoyance of the ship and sea patterned shower-curtain sucking towards his legs, is cancelled out by the pleasure of a little-girl-story.

One night, he tips a whole mug of coffee with milk and honey, over the pages where the story is written in black texta. Almost every word is obliterated. In a rush he pulls his portable typewriter from its old green case and begins to type the story out as best he recollects. Suddenly he's no longer certain of how the words go. Maybe he's adding things.

The old age fairy, funny to think, is also the tooth fairy who flies in yore window at night and gets yore tooth from under yore pillow. Shes got long clever fingers and sits next to yore sleeping head whilst her arm reaches under to take baby teeth away forever. Except for one tooth left at the bottom row, shes got all of mine. All up she payed two hundred and twenty cents to me witch isnt much. *Yore so grone up is what my Dad Eric says* each time he sees me. I show with my tongue the gaps where my teeth were. The old age fairy is a gentle one. She sits there on the pillow and whispers things to keep me happy and smiling. When once I tried to trick her and hid a tooth in a matchbox where I kept my nipsy beetle I felt her wings tapping me. Next morning there was a 20 cents in the matchbox and my beetle and tooth was gone. It's a clever fairy. She wears a dress. Underneath, she preens her feathers with her long fingers.

People don't know but she keeps on visiting you even after the last baby tooths gone. *Are the years adding up gently,* she asks everyone in their sleep and if yore getting really old or getting that way, she'll start knocking out yore real teeth not yore baby teeth and she wont leave any money for those. Eric my Dad lost one and the Dentist Dickson put a plastic one instead but it wont trick the fairy you know that. Theres probably more old age fairies than I can think of but its the tooth one I know best.

Other old things are clothes. When Mum used to think one of Dad's shirts was too old she'd say the *materials so thin you could shoot peas through it.*

Old age is a shipreck said Grandma Gilson who ort to know and whose mother sailed here in a boat from England where my other Grandma is still alive. *I'm as old as the hills* was all she would say if I asked. When she died it was a storm and Dad said the angels were playing crowcay with her. I didn't see the joke. From our house there's lots more houses and then the lumpy hills. I dont think it was those hills my gran meant. Her and Mr Ertle were the oldest people I've ever ever known.

At school yore as old as yore skin or the hair on yore head. *Time is a freckle past a mole on your rist.* At the turn of the century I worked out I will be 26 years old.

Mum says I'll want to use makeup when I'm a bit older but I dont think so.

Old roses fall apart with a wind or a finger touching them. Bindies cant get through my feet the skin is so old an tough.

Only the old age fairy never grows old. Her tears are the

dew on the grass in the morning shes so unhappy making
people ugly and sadder. Really she would just like to do the
little ones. They are happy to lose their teeth and find the
money under the pillow.

Using two fingers, Eric Gilson taps out his memory onto
A4 Bond Cartridge. He tries to resurrect all the quaint
spelling errors and turns of expression but he thinks he
has exaggerated the childishness of his daughter's story. Only the teacher's comment, written in some sort of
indestructible ink, has survived the flood of coffee and
Eric's not interested in that. In fact at the time Jessica
was handed back her story, with no gold stars and lots
of red pen through it, Eric had felt it cause enough to
pay a visit to the teacher. The teacher turned out to be a
traditional and even to Eric, rather formidable man,
who reminded him of his old scripture teacher. Perhaps
there was something biblical shared in their pinched up
pronouncements.

'Yes Mr Gilson, I concede your point that Jessica's
story is very creative and interesting but you can see for
yourself she's backward for her age in spelling and
punctuation.'

'Well, I hardly think backward is the right word.'

'Now I know you and Mrs Gilson aren't together at
the moment and we do take this into consideration
when assessing Jessica's performance.'

'It was a very amicable separation, Mr Stewart.'

'Yes, but I don't think you realize Mr Gilson, that
over a quarter of the children here are from a broken
home. We learn to pick the signs. A certain deteriora-
tion in attention, a lack of progress in the simple things
like spelling.'

'I hardly think my marriage breaking up has anything
to do with my daughter's spelling!'

'Well, she's obviously disturbed. I was going to contact you about this anyway. After I collected the books
for marking last week, I saw that Jessica had ripped out

the story we're talking about and that previous work already marked, had had gold stars added. Up to eight gold stars she'd given herself, whereas I only ever give three at most. And I certainly didn't give her any for the effort you're talking about.'

'Actually Mr Stewart,' confesses Eric to himself and the room, staring at his typewriter, 'it was me who put in the fucking stars and ripped out the story. But if I'd told you that then you'd really have thought I was a stuffed up father.' He is silent then, thinking of the expression 'broken home'. It makes him remember the last parent teacher night he and Janice went to in the same car. The windows of the classroom were decorated with all the kids' houses. Our Happy Home, Jessica had written under hers. 'Broken Home,' makes Eric think of all those bright paint walls cracking and the safe looking chimneys toppling down.

Eric groans and swivels his ergonomic chair away from the desk. He trundles into his kitchen and still sitting perched on the velvet seat, makes himself more coffee and five pieces of toast and vegemite with thick butter. Tonight he's too depressed to be worrying about heart disease, hardening arteries. In the kitchen, so obviously designed for midgets, he can't fry an egg without clunking his head on the beaten copper exhaust hood. Despite ergonomics, he's crouching his back to relieve a twinge of pain. Someone in the street plays a slightly stretched Rolling Stones album. *Baby, baby, baby you're out of time*. The notes thin and flatten inside his head. Abruptly he leaves his chair and goes to an untidy brick and plank bookshelf. He plonks five books of quotations onto the coffee table and starts to look up old age in the Pan Dictionary of Contemporary Quotations. He flicks it shut. Inside on the white title page, his wife has written, 'Happy 38th Darling. Will you still need me, will you still feed me, when I'm 64?'

He opens the book again and finds the section on ageing. He reads, *It's sad to grow old but nice to ripen:*

Brigitte Bardot. Eric thinks of the flush on a peach or a pear. Although in the Women's Day magazine he read in the dentist's waiting room, Brigitte Bardot hadn't looked luscious at all. More like a last season apple, wrinkling at the curves. When Eric thinks of himself ripening, he can only picture a black splotching banana with a soft brown mush inside.

On the wings of the morning they gather and fly
In the hush of the night time I hear them go by
The horses of memory thundering through
With flashing white fetlocks all wet with the dew.

Will H Ogilvie. Eric recites the ballad aloud. Jessica wants to ride horses. The old man from the flat in Alla-wah put the idea into her head and she won't let it rest. He turns back to the book of quotations.

As one gets older one loses the sense of fiction. Fiction is something linked with youth: François Truffaut. Eric would like to yell that quote in Mr Stewart's stern face.

Children are the best story tellers. Only children or old people can imagine the worlds behind cracks in the wall. Eric believes this but wonders where he fits in. Recently he saw Truffaut's 'The Woman Next Door' and didn't enjoy its passion nearly as much as the twenty three year old who doesn't like to hold hands with him in public. Not even in dark public places. Eric's indifference to the film continues to worry him but not as much as the twenty three year old's indifference towards himself. He longs to cuddle against her in the nights she stays, to curve himself into her warm bottom. However he can always sense her tension, until in sleep she rolls out of his arm to the edge of the bed.

When Jessica stays, he lets her sleep in his bed. She wears blue polka dot pyjamas. When she wakes him in the morning he calls her his blue flannel sheep dog and they romp for a while. Just like old times, almost. On these mornings, Eric notices how his daughter's hair gets all mussed up around her ears, like Janice's used to before her morning shower. The twenty three year old girlfriend wakes like a film star, hair rumpled only enough to make her round, smooth cheeks more alluring.

Eric pulls his fingers through his hair. It's greasy and too long round his ears. He sighs, melodramatic in an empty room and goes into the kitchen to peel a shiny, first of the season, Delicious apple. He shines the fruit against his chest. The skin is dappled red and green. It spindles and springs like a toy in his fingers. Outside he sees the small trees are shedding a mixture of red and black berries. Where people have trodden them into the cement footpath, they are like the tracks of a bleeding animal or person. Eric shakes his head. He can hardly believe his gloom when tomorrow Jessica will be arriving.

His daughter's goodnight kisses repel and attract him. Butterfly kisses she calls them, with her eyelashes fluttering on his nose. So provocative, but that is his construction not the child's. He is full of a desire to knead his wife's small buttocks and feel her going to sleep against his chest. Is it the role of protector he is pining for, he asks himself rhetorically. For he is longing to encase a small and obliging body in his long thin arms. There are a multitude of old age and evil fairies working on Eric gently. More frequently now he can feel their light and seductive fingers. He bites hard into the tart apple that is so young it is bleeding from the core.